Tad had been leaning back in the chair and now sat forward with a bang. "You need a lesson in manners."

"Not from you," I said. I did some fast figuring. There was three Wilsons between me and the front door.

"Boys?" Tad said.

Bob and Buck began walking toward me. I felt under the counter for the truncheon Mr. Levy kept there. The two of them came behind the counter, one on each side, with me in the middle. I quick grabbed the truncheon and swung out, hitting Buck just below the jaw and knocking him backward. Then I rounded on Bob and found myself staring into the barrel of a six-gun. Bob had this crazy smile on his face as he pulled back the hammer.

THE
Second Gun

James Clifton Cobb

BERKLEY BOOKS, NEW YORK

THE SECOND GUN

A Berkley Book / published by arrangement with
the author

PRINTING HISTORY
Berkley edition / December 2000

All rights reserved.
Copyright © 2000 by Joshua Dann
Cover illustration by Bruce Emmett

The Penguin Putnam Inc. World Wide Web site address is
http://www.penguinputnam.com

ISBN: 0-425-17739-4

BERKLEY®
Berkley Books are published by The Berkley Publishing Group,
a division of Penguin Putnam Inc.,
375 Hudson Street, New York, New York 10014.
BERKLEY and the "B" design
are trademarks belonging to Penguin Putnam Inc.

PRINTED IN THE UNITED STATES OF AMERICA

10 9 8 7 6 5 4 3 2 1

1

IF IT HADN'T been for Gentleman Jake Murchison, I'd
be dead right now. Well, not just right now. I'd be dead
startin' April 6, 1881, and continue bein' dead right on
through now into the forever after. Always be exact, Jake
used to say. That's what made him the greatest lawman
in Arizona, maybe the world. And he could always tell
when someone was lying, too. I knew it, 'cause I'd watch
his mustache. He had this big old handlebar stacheroo,
and it'd twitch, just a frog's hair up and to the right.

Anyways, the night I met Gentleman Jake, I was
sweepin' up the hay and cigar butts and gobs a tobacco
goobers that didn't quite make it into the cuspidor. That
was my job, see. I wasn't but fifteen year old, no other
blood in the world 'cept what was under my skin, and I
had this job as stable boy and sweeper-upper at the
Granger Saloon and Tryer Luck Casino. That was a play
on words, there, Tryer Luck. The saloon, and everything
else in Granger, was owned by Tom Tryer, see, and he
called it—the gambling part—Tryer Luck. Get it?

I'm sweepin' up the joint even though it's payday crowded, and the bartender, Ike Hawkins, is pullin' beers as fast as the ranch hands and silver miners can throw down their nickels. He wipes off the bar with a towel and throws it at my ear. He did that a lot. Never when I was lookin', see, 'cause I'd catch it or duck. Just when I wasn't. That may sound funny to you, but a wet towel has some weight behind it, and it would sting. He'd throw the towel at me, and I'd toss it in a pile that I'd have to wash later. When he hit me a good one, he'd ring this bell over back of the bar, and that'd hand everybody a good laugh. I got so I didn't pay it no mind.

When Jake first come in, you couldn't tell right away he was a dude. He wasn't wearing no ruffled shirt or nothin', he just looked like he'd been on the trail a while like anybody else passing through. But I noticed something about him right away, so I kept track of him out of the corner of my eye while I swept. He was a big fellow, probably an inch or two over six feet, and he looked strong. He had these cold blue eyes that did most of his talking for him. When he did talk at all, you had to strain a little to hear him, and he didn't care because he never talked any louder than that.

First of all, this drunk miner gives him a bump, like fellows always do to a stranger in a saloon, kind of take their measure.

This miner bumps him and then stands back, kind of facing Jake down. Jake just rolled his eyes.

"Watch it there!" The miner said.

It was hard to hear Jake's answer, because he spoke so low, but I made it my business to sweep nearby just so's I could catch it.

"Shut up," Jake said. He didn't say it loud or angry.

Just sort of matter-of-fact, the way you'd brush a flea off a horse.

Well, sir, that miner didn't know what-all to do. I think he got the impression that he'd bit off a little more'n he could chew, so he didn't do nothing. He just pretended he'd never said nothing to Jake and went back to the bar and ordered a beer.

Jake shook his head, kind amused-like, as if he'd just seen somebody get hit in the butt with a saloon door. Then he walked over to the bar, near where I was sweeping. Next thing I know, Jake's arm goes up, and he quick catches the towel meant for my left ear.

"This yours?" Jake says with a little grin.

"Yessir," says I, "thankee." But I'm also a little embarrassed, because Ike is starin' daggers at me, like it was my fault somebody else catched the towel.

Jake went over to the bar and called for a beer. Ike give him this cold look he had a way of doing, this look that could make a rattlesnake go mind his own business. But Jake paid him no mind, just took a nickel from his pocket and put it on the bar. Ike drew him a beer, all right, but he slammed it down on the bar so hard that half of it flew out of the glass.

I'm watchin' real careful now, 'cause the last thing anyone wants is Ike mad at them. I seen him throw four miners out the door once, one right after t'other. So I'm curious what Jake'll do.

Well, sir, all he did was shrug his shoulders a little. Then, real slow-like, he took his nickel off the bar, put it back in his pocket. Then he took out two pennies and put them on the bar.

You could've heard a pin drop. The piano player was on a break, so it wasn't like the piano stopped playing, but the fellows nearby all turned to watch. I'm secret rooting for the stranger to knock Ike's block off, but I also know that there's really no good can come out of beating up a bartender. Still, I'm watching.

But it was just at that time the swinging doors crashed open and in come the Wilson brothers. Course, they never just come in. They were hootin' and a-hollerin' and pushing and shoving. Their daddy owned the biggest ranch in these parts plus a piece of one of the mines, so they always had plenty a money. But like a lot of sons of hardworking men who get rich, they were a bunch of wastrels. There were five of them: Bob, the oldest; then Tad; then Buck; then Earl; then Virge. Virge was the youngest, only eighteen, and the most useless of all. He'd start in with someone, and if they looked like they could lick him, and just about anybody could, he'd quick whistle for his brothers. The others were pretty strong but mostly stupid. 'Cepting Tad. I was always a little scared of Tad, because he wasn't only mean, he was also smart, which to me has always been a scary combination. He could quick figure out what somebody's weakness was and go after it, and worse, he was the fastest draw in these parts.

As usual when they come in, everybody in the place set to makin' themselves real small, 'cause you never knew who they were gonna pick on next. Once they pulled my pants down and threw me into the street. The girls who wasn't upstairs made a beeline out of there. I heard the girls talkin' once about how them damn Wilsons liked to hurt them.

I noticed that Jake was paying strict attention, and I could see his mind working. It struck me funny, but I could almost hear him inside his head, sizing them up and finally figurin' on Tad as being the one to reckon with.

Anyhow, I was so concerned about the stranger having to mix it up with the Wilsons that I plum forgot all about yours truly. I forgot to make myself inconspicuous-like, and Virge was the first one to notice. He snuck up behind me and shoved me so hard I fell right on the floor.

Everybody started to laugh, but it was that fake laugh people do when someone they're afraid of does something he thinks is funny. The Wilsons themselves laughed hardest of all, especially Earl, who was big and fat and had this high-pitch yowl sounded like a pig with his foot caught.

Then Virge grabs up my broom from where I dropped it and starts makin' like he's sweepin' me up.

"Why, Nate," he says to me, fake-friendly, "I'm jest helpin' you out here!" And that made his brothers laugh all the more.

You ever get so mad you just want to hit something or someone, and hang the consequences? It usually comes from being made a fool of, I've found. Well, when old Virge started in with the broom, all I knew was I wanted to smash his face in, and I didn't even think about his brothers. I was always strong for my age, and anyhow, you didn't have to be real strong to be able to whip Virge.

Well, sir, the next time Virge touched me with that broom—he always did let a joke go on too long—I jumped up and punched him smack in the nose, just as hard as ever I could. It made a noise, too, a kind of a pop. Then Virge went right down on his behind, and here it gets funny, or at least I thought so. He had this surprised look on his face. Then he put his hand to his nose, saw all the blood, and started cryin' like a baby for his mama's milk.

It was pretty funny, and I started to laugh. That is, until

I noticed that I was the only one in the whole place who was laughin'. Then I shut up real quick.

The Wilsons all had these dangerous looks on their faces, especially Tad, who had a scowl would of made the devil hisself tryin' to make things up to him. He looked me square in the eye and said, "Well now, you're gonna pay for that 'un."

I knew I was sunk. I never was a churchgoer, but I started believin' right quick about then, prayin' the Lord that whatever they did wouldn't hurt too much nor take too long.

The Wilsons started walking toward me, real slow, and I just stood there, not doing much of anything. They got real close when someone stepped in their path, blocking off their view of me.

It was Jake.

"Out of our way, fellow," Tad said. "Our quarrel ain't with you."

"I do believe it is," Jake said. "But it needn't be. I can buy you all a beer and we can forget the whole thing. I'd take that course of action, if I were you."

No one had ever heard a stranger talk so flowery before, and it set everyone to howling. Everyone, that is, except Tad.

"There's five of us, fellow," Tad said.

Jake looked at Virge, who was still mewling on the floor. "Looks like four to me, friend," Jake said.

"I ain't your friend," Tad said.

"That's a shame, but I'll get over it. Beer for the boys," he added over his shoulder to Ike.

"We'll buy our own beer," Tad says.

The stranger shook his head, not like he was disagreein'

with anybody, but more sad-like. "You really want a fight?" he asked Tad.

Tad didn't say nothing, he just pulled his coat back to show his six-gun.

"Hold on there," Jake said. "I don't have a gun."

That caused quite some consternation in the place. How could a fellow ride the trail without no gun?

"You ain't got a gun?" Earl yelped.

"I've got a Henry rifle hitched in my saddle, but I don't have a pistol."

"Why ain't you got no six-gun?" Buck demanded.

"Don't like 'em. The Henry suits me fine."

Tad was fed up with all the discussion. He grabbed Buck's Army Colt from his holster and tossed it high in the air toward Jake. And then the damnedest thing happened.

Jake caught the pistol on the fly, and without even bothering to steady or aim it, he loosed off the six fastest shots any human being could possibly do. The first knocked off Tad's hat. Then, as Tad was reaching for his own gun, Jake put the other five shots right into Tad's pistol before it even cleared the holster.

Well, sir, them shots was still echoin', but other than that it got so quiet you coulda heard a mouse belch. And here's where it gets interesting.

Most men, when they find out they're up against someone who can shoot like Jake, well, they back off. Any other fella, after seeing what Jake could do, woulda said, "Well, there, pardner, I guess I'll be on my way," or even, "Say, that beer you was offerin'? Think I'll take you up on it just now."

But not Tad. Tad was the sort who never knew when to quit and never gave up on nothing. He looked at his own gun, which was all messed up on account a what five bullets done to it, and shouted, "You owe me a new gun, damn you!"

Jake gave his head a little shake, like he'd been slogged and needed to clear it. Then he tossed back the empty gun. "There you are," he said.

Tad caught the gun with an angry snap of his hand and shoved it over to Buck. "That ain't what I mean," Tad said. "That ain't my gun. You owe me one."

Jake did something funny. He turned his head so that he was facing most of the folks in the bar and said, "Is this fellow all right in the head?"

The men tried not to laugh, but it was tough, and wound up sounding like a big fart.

"You tellin' me I'm crazy?" Tad shouted.

"No," Jake said. "I was telling *them* you're crazy."

Tad didn't know what to say to that, and neither did anyone else. Then Jake said something I didn't understand.

"Pearls," he said to no one in particular. "I'm casting pearls."

Course he must a meant something else, because I didn't see no necklace anyplace.

"I'm a-callin' you out," Tad shouted.

Jake then made a little face, the sort you make if all of a sudden someone says something that might as well be in Greek.

"How can you call me out twice?" Jake wanted to know. "I already beat you once."

"I'll say when I'm done," Tad said.

Jake thought this over for a minute. Then he said, real quiet-like, "Fellow, I've grown a little tired of you. Now, we can go out there and draw, and I'll kill you. Or we can square off like men . . . with these." He held up two fair-sized mitts.

For the first time, Tad got a little edgy. He was mean and fast, but he was nowhere near as strong as Jake.

"Aw, hell, Tad," Earl said. "I'll take him on and whup him."

Just to show you the kind a guy Jake was, he coulda said something like, "Oh, you're a coward and you need someone else to fight for you," or something like that, since Earl was the strongest of the brothers. But all Jake did was nod, as if to it say it made no never-mind to him which Wilson he fought.

Well, sir, about a second after Jake nodded his head, the place went flooey. Everybody started whoopin' and placin' bets and yelling out drink orders to Ike, who looked like a octopus his arms were moving so fast pulling beers and filling whiskey glasses.

You'd a thought it was gonna be the fight of the century. Earl's brothers helped him off with his coat and started rubbing on his arms and shoulders and giving him all sorts of advice that he didn't need and wasn't going to follow. Earl could knock a horse down with his fists.

"Could I trouble you to hang on to this for a bit?" Jake asked me, holding out his coat.

"Yes, sir," I said.

Jake handed me the coat and went through the doors after the Wilsons, rolling up his sleeves.

The whole saloon emptied out into the street, and soon there was a giant circle. It took near fifteen minutes for everyone to be ready. Men kept running out from the saloon balancing drinks and shouting, "Wait fer me! Don't start yet!"

Finally, it was all set. Earl shook off a final word from

Buck and stepped in the middle. There weren't no referee, because we didn't have no town marshal at the time. Jake went up to Earl and stuck out his hand, like they was gentlemen, but Earl just spat. Then the two squared off.

I never before seen no one square off the way Jake did. Most fellas hold their dukes upwards with their elbows facing downwards. Not Jake. His elbows went more to the sides; his right fist was in close to his chest and the left up near chin level and farther out. His jaw he dropped to his shoulder. I saw some fellas in the crowd imitate it— not like they was making fun of Jake but more trying it themselves.

Earl went at Jake and took a huge swing at him with his right. If he'd a caught Jake, it woulda been good night. But Jake just ducked. It weren't really a duck, more of a downward move sideways. He did it from the waist, and it was real quick, without moving his feet at all. I never seen nothing so smooth from a man that big.

What Jake did next surprised everybody. Instead of moving away, he went carefully toward Earl, and this is what he did. He'd punch Earl in the gut with his left, punches so fast you could hardly see them. Then one big one with his right. It sounds slow when you talk about it, but believe me, it weren't. More like a boom-boom-*bam!* Boom-boom-*bam!*

He just kept doing that. Earl didn't know what-all to do with his hands. He couldn't lay a finger on Jake, because no matter how hard he tried, Jake either weren't there or else blocked him.

I couldn't help but notice that Jake never once touched Earl's face. He just kept hitting him in the same place, right around Earl's big blubber. I'd a thought Jake would be getting tired, but I didn't even see him break a sweat.

He knew how to pace himself. After he'd slog on Earl for a while, he'd move backward and let Earl chase him. Course, Earl couldn't touch him, not the way Jake did that bending trick. Earl would tucker himself out right quick going after Jake, and then Jake would move right on back in and start punching on him again.

Earl started huffin' and puffin', and I saw that his big arms didn't seem to have no strength left. He could hardly even lift them up anymore. When Jake saw that, he slowed down and concentrated on a couple big slogs. *Wham! Wham! Wham! Wham!* Everybody kinda let out a breath with each one, because Earl would sort of jump every time Jake hit him. Nobody'd seen anyone ever strong enough to do that to Earl.

And in the middle of the last one, Earl went down. He dropped to his knees and then tried to get up but fell on his hands instead. His hands couldn't hold him up, and down he went for good.

Just to show you how scared the Wilsons had everybody, after Earl went down, the men just stood there. Nobody moved nor said a word while the Wilsons went over and helped Earl up. I could see that Jake wanted to go over to them and be a good sport about it, but Tad stood and hollered, "This ain't over yet!"

Jake spread his hands and did that head-clearing thing I would come to know. Then he turned to me.

"I'll take that coat of mine, young fellow," he said.

"Yes, sir," I said. Jake made like he was going into his pocket to give me a tip, but I cut him off. "That's all right, sir," I said. "That fight was worth whatever you were going to give me."

Jake smiled at me. It was a real man-to-man smile, the kind you can tell don't come easy and means a lot when it does. I couldn't help it, but I felt sorta proud of myself for having earned it.

When at last the Wilsons were mounted up and on their way, the crowd exploded and began gathering around Jake, slapping his back and trying to shake his hand. You could tell the whole spectacle irritated Jake, and he made for his own horse. I guess he was about as entertained by our little town as he was ever going to be.

"Excuse me, stranger, I wonder if I might have a word." It was Mr. Levy, who was the mayor and the owner of the town's general store. Mr. Levy hadn't wanted to be mayor, but since he was one of the only men in town who didn't kowtow to the Wilsons and who everyone said was also the only honest man in town, he was elected anyway. I knew Mr. Levy's daughter, Rebecca, who was my age and prettier than a buttercup. I couldn't figure it, but whenever I saw her, my tongue got five times as thick, and my heart would start pounding out of my chest. Not that it mattered; she was way too good for a stable boy.

"My name's Levy," he said. After a pause, he added in a sort of embarrassed way, "I'm the mayor around here."

"You have my condolences," Jake replied. I didn't know what condolences were, but from Mr. Levy's broad smile, I could tell that he liked what Jake had said. "Jake Murchison, Mr. Mayor," he said, and the two shook hands.

"Mr. Murchison, I have a proposition for you."

"I'm on my way to California, Mayor, and I haven't time for propositions."

"Fair enough. I'll come right to the point, then you can be on your way. This is a boomtown, Mr. Murchison. Now, that can be good or bad. Right now, it's bad. We've no law and order here, sir. Having had your mettle tested before one and all, would you consider accepting a post as town marshal?"

"With all due respect, Mayor, I have just considered it . . . and dismissed it."

The talk was pretty formal, but you could see they were both enjoying it. "Out of hand?" Mr. Levy asked.

Jake regarded Mr. Levy. "Mayor, you seem like a fellow who can handle himself. Why don't *you* be the town marshal?"

Mr. Levy seemed stumped for a moment. He couldn't say a word. It was as though he had an idea, but the words wouldn't come.

"Thanks for the offer," Jake said, swinging onto his horse. "And good luck to you."

"I haven't answered your question, Mr. Murchison."

Jake wheeled his horse and looked expectantly at Mr. Levy.

"Because *I'm* not an experienced lawman, and *you* are," Mr. Levy said forcefully.

The words seemed to hit Jake in the face like one of Earl's misdirected punches. He sagged in his saddle.

"Aw, hell," he groaned. "Goddamn it to hell."

2

I CAN'T TELL you why, but when Mr. Levy extended an invitation to supper at his home, he included me. Mr. Levy was that kind of fellow. At first I thought Mr. Levy only asked because I happened to be right there, and he was afraid of hurting my feelings.

"Much obliged, Mr. Levy, but I got sweepin' up to do," I said to give him an out.

"Nonsense, Nathaniel," he said, "you look like you could use a good meal."

"Come along, son," Jake said quietly. "Any second of mine deserves a good dinner."

I didn't know what a second was, but I was sure glad to be one. I was also a little anxious, 'cause Rebecca would be there. I figured I'd watch Jake and do exactly what he did.

The first thing you noticed about Mr. Levy's house was how clean it was. The whole place sparkled and smelled like good food and clean linen. The table was set with shiny new plates and silver, and there were two candles and bread I never seen before. It looked like it was a buncha thick braids all baked together.

Mrs. Levy looked like a growed-up version of Rebecca, tall and slim with bright green eyes and dark red hair. When she smiled, it was like the whole room suddenly got brighter.

"I'm so glad you could join us, Nathaniel," she said, and I got real warm all over. I never knew my own ma, but I hoped she was something like Mrs. Levy.

I felt a slight punch on the back of my shoulder. "Hey, Nate!" It was Rebecca, looking pretty darn bright herself.

"Rebecca!" Mrs. Levy cautioned. "Is that a way to treat a guest in our home?"

"Awwwwfully sorry, Mumsy," Rebecca said, changing her voice to something high 'n mighty. Rebecca could make her voice sound like anybody she wanted it to. "Welcome to our humble chateau, Nathaniel. Won't you sit down," she added snootily.

I didn't know what a chateau was, but I guessed I was in one. Anyway, I was going to be sitting next to Rebecca, so I figured I'd best not act like a nincompoop.

"Mr. Murchison," Mrs. Levy greeted Jake, "please sit down here." So that was the arrangement: Mr. and Mrs. Levy at the head and foot of the table, Jake on one side, and me and Rebecca on t'other.

There were wineglasses for all of us, though me and Rebecca's was only a splash. Mr. Levy held up his glass, thanked the Lord for it, and then allowed as he was happy to announce the appointment of Mr. Murchison as the new town marshal. He was going to send to Prescott for a new badge tomorrow, he said.

We all drank, and then Mrs. Levy thanked the Lord for that braided bread, after which she passed it around and we each took off a chunk. I never tasted nothing like it; it was moist and sort of sweet, but not too sweet. I looked over at Rebecca and had a funny idea: I thought, if I married her, why, I could eat this kind of bread whenever I wanted.

I felt like everyone was watchin' me, even though they wasn't. I had never ate in anyone's house before. Ever since I could remember, I took my bowl and my spoon and a glass of milk out in the stable. But I knew somehow this'd be different, so I watched Jake real careful. We had this soup, see, this heavenly chicken soup with vegetables and a big ball a dough right in the middle. I et it like Jake did, 'stead a my usual shoveling it in. I held my spoon between my fingers like he did, and didn't slurp it but kinda dipped small spoonfuls into my mouth.

But here's where I'm real proud a myself. Just like Jake, I used my knife and fork for everything, cutting small pieces and not switching the fork to my right hand. And I was rewarded for it, too.

"Why, Nathaniel, your manners are excellent," Mrs. Levy said, and I got that damned glow again. Rebecca looked at me and batted her eyelids and mouthed "Wonderful."

I was a little surprised that Mr. Levy and Jake didn't talk no business at dinner. They spoke mostly of where they came from. Mr. and Mrs. Levy both came from Germany when they were small children. They lived in Philadelphia, and then they moved west just after Rebecca was born, right after the war. Mr. Levy had been in a Pennsylvania regiment, and said something about a fresh start in a new, unspoiled place. Jake nodded and said he had been just a little too young, and Mr. Levy replied, "You ought to thank God for that."

Jake said he was from New York, and Mr. Levy allowed as he figured as much. Jake also said he remembered the draft riots in New York, and then pardoned himself for bringing up such an ugly matter at the table and quick changed the subject. He asked if Rebecca was named after the heroine in *Ivanhoe*, and Mrs. Levy brightened and said why, yes, and in fact, the real-life Rebecca from who Sir Walter Scott took the name was also from Philadelphia.

And then something funny happened. Something that changed my whole life right then and there.

"I feel terrible!" Mrs. Levy exclaimed, all of a sudden. "We've been ignoring our young guest! Nathaniel? What about you?"

"Ma'am?" I said, feeling on the spot.

"What do you plan to do?"

"You mean . . . now?"

She laughed, but not in a mean way. "No, dear."

I don't know where this came from, because I'd never thought of it before. It just kinda popped out.

"I been savin' up, ma'am."

"Well, that's wonderful! For some land?"

"No ma'am. I been saving up to buy a piece of Mr. Wilson's mine."

You'd a thought I just told the world's funniest joke the way they burst out laughing. I felt myself getting a little red with embarrassment, but Mr. Levy patted me on the shoulder. "We're not laughing at you, boy," he said. "I had a feeling you were ambitious."

Well, I knew what that meant, and I understood why they would think that way. I was, after all, just a sweeper-upper and stable boy.

Jake looked over at me and winked, not a sly wink, but one that seemed to say, "Good for you."

For a second I got a little lost in myself. I really did buy into Wilson's mine, and I really did have a swell house like this one, and best of all, I really was married to Rebecca.

"The boy really should go to school and learn how to read," Mrs. Levy was saying.

The back of my neck got hot. "I can read," I said shortly.

"You can? Where'd you learn?" Rebecca asked.

There was a girl, a few years back, one of the saloon girls, named Mabel. She taught me the beginnings. I don't know what happened to her; the girls usually just move along after awhile. I remembered her, though. She always looked at me kind of sad, and acted sweet to me. Maybe she had a boy of her own, once.

Anyhow, the rest I just picked up.

"You can read?" Rebecca challenged me.

"Yes, I can read, Rebecca."

She turned around and grabbed a book off a shelf behind the table. She opened it to no place in particular. "Then read this!"

"Rebecca!" her father said sternly.

"I just want to see if he can." She shrugged.

I looked down at the page. It was English, but only just. "I might get the words wrong," I warned her. "It ain't proper English."

"Neither is 'ain't,' " Rebecca said smugly.

"All right," I sighed.

"Methought that I had broken from the Tower,
And was embarkt to cross to Burgundy;

And, in my company, my brother Gloster;
Who from my cabin tempted me to walk—"

"How did you do that?" Rebecca demanded.

"Do what?" I wanted to know. All I did was read.

"You just looked at it once! And only for a second!"

"Oh." I sighed in relief. "I always do that. That's how I read."

"You've read it before," Rebecca insisted. "You know it by heart!"

"I never even seen this before, much less read it," I argued.

"Nate?" Mrs. Levy asked. "Would you read us the rest?"

Rebecca slammed her hand over the page so I couldn't see it. I took a deep breath and gave it a try.

"Who from my cabin tempted me to walk
Upon the hatches: thence we lookt toward England,
and cited up a thousand heavy times,
During the wars of York and Lancaster,
That had befaln us. As we paced along
The giddy footing of the hatches,
Methought that Gloster stumbled; and, in falling,
Struck me, that thought to stay him, overboard,
Into the tumbling billows of the main.
Lord, Lord! methought, what pain it was to
Drown!"

I stopped and noticed that Jake and Mr. Levy had been listening with their eyes half-shut. Even stranger, Mrs. Levy had a single tear streak down her cheek.

Jake seemed like someone just woke him up. *"Richard*

III," he said, nodding. He looked at me but pointed to Rebecca. "Give him something else," he said.

Rebecca flipped to another page and held it up to my face. "All right?" she asked softly.

"I think so," I said.

> *"Then plainly know my heart's dear love is set*
> *On the fair daughter of rich Capulet:*
> *As mine on hers, so hers is set on mine;*
> *And all combined, save what thou must combine*
> *By holy marriage: when, where and how,*
> *We met, we wooed—"*

"Rebecca!" Mrs. Levy shook her head.

"What?" Rebecca said, all innocent-like.

"Gentlemen?" Mr. Levy said. "Cigars. You too, Nate."

I got up and started clearing my place, but Mrs. Levy stopped me. "You're a good boy, Nathaniel," she said. "Go join the men."

"You're sure?" I said. I never et a meal where I didn't have to clean up after myself.

"Go on," she said softly.

"It's remarkable," Mr. Levy was saying to Jake, "how much you've spoken this evening and how little you've actually told me about yourself."

Jake shrugged. "I don't like to talk about myself," Jake said.

"You were a lawman," Mr. Levy reminded him.

"Yes, I was."

"Tell me about it." He put up his hands like he didn't mean nothing by it. "It needn't go further than this room."

"I'll keep it short," Jake said.

As it turned out, he didn't keep it as short as all that. Jake's people were well-to-do merchants in New York City. Jake had gone to West Point and graduated, but a few years later, he found that army life wasn't for him. He quit and came back to New York, where they was starting a new police force. With his army experience, he became the youngest police president in the city. His district was a place called Five Corners, which he guessed had more thieves, murderers, pimps, and other no-good scum than any other place on earth. There were places made the Tryer Luck Casino look like a nursery, he said. There was drunk, opiumed, stabbed, and shot people just lyin' in the street, it seemed like. Jake did his best, but it was a thankless job.

"What made you decide to leave?" Mr. Levy asked.

"Another time," Jake said. "It was purely my decision."

"Has it something to do with your not carrying a pistol?"

"Another time," Jake repeated.

"All right," Mr. Levy said. "The job pays one hundred twenty-five dollars a month. We'll also get your board at Zeb Stanton's hotel. And," he added with a grin, "all the freeloading at my store you can handle. We'll start with a new six-gun. I've got a Colt Army revolver that ought to do the job."

"I'd rather not," Jake said.

"I'd rather you did," Mr. Levy said, bristling a little. "I'd prefer you had one and didn't use it, than went without when you might need it."

Jake closed his eyes and shook his head. "Very well," he said. "What about young Nate here? We can't let a man of his talents spend his life cleaning spittoons."

"Of course not," Mr. Levy agreed. "Nathaniel? Would

you like to come to work for me? In my shop?"

It took all I had not to jump up and flip backward and shout, "Hell, yes!" But I didn't. All I did was nod my head and say, "Yes, sir. I believe I'd like that just fine."

I had worked for Tom Tryer ever since I could remember, and I thought to make our parting of the ways a bit more polite, but the truth was, Tom never paid me no mind to begin with. All he ever said about me was, "Nate wasn't born, he jes' got left somewheres." Still, I thought I owed it to him to tell him of my appreciation for his keeping me off the streets over the years, kind of gentleman-like, but Ike wouldn't let me get in to see him. He just said, "Well, you're quittin', then get out."

It kinda bugged me at first, but the truth was, Tom had always treated me like a dog anyhow, and I was damn near thrilled to pieces to be shut of old Ike. Ike was the kind of fellow you hoped might not be all that bad at the bottom, but he was every bit as much a snake there as at the top.

So I was free of the Granger Saloon and Tryer Luck Casino. Mr. Levy asked me what I expected to be paid, and I told him what Tom·Tryer had give me. He made this surprised snort and started to say, "Why, that low-down—" but then he stopped real quick. Then he said he'd give me twice what old Tom had, and he arranged for me to room at Zeb Stanton's, same as Jake. Course, Jake's room was the best in the house, and mine was next to the kitchen, but it suited me just fine. There wasn't no straw nor horse dung, and I had a real bed and a wash-bowl. The best thing was, I had my very own pot right under the bed; no more gettin' up and hikin' to the privy in the dead of winter.

Of course, I worked my butt off for Mr. Levy, harder even than when I was at the saloon. The difference was, Mr. Levy never threw no wet towel at my ear. I don't mean just that, but I felt . . . well, better about things. And I felt a little more important. Not like I was better than anybody else, but at least as good. Like Mr. Levy was glad I was there.

I also noticed something about Mr. Levy right away. He always charged less than what the sign said. Especially if the customer really looked strapped for cash. Like the first day. This family come in lookin' all bedraggled. You could tell they'd come clear across the country. That wasn't no rare thing in those days; our town seemed to be a crossroads for the whole world. Folks came heading south for Mexico, north to Wyoming, east from California and especially west. Those heading west were mostly from the South. Lots of poor Southerners went west in the years after the war because they just couldn't make a go of things at home anymore. Not after what the war done to their end of the country. And our part of Arizona was decidedly Southern in its sympathies.

So this family comes in. The papa, he had a wooden leg, and there was his tired-looking wife and four little kids. Outside they had an old wagon and two horses looked more tired than they did. You could see this was their last stop before their destination, which the papa said was a place in California called Vy-salia. They picked out their supplies: oats for the horses, coffee, jerky beef, flour, a little sugar, stuff like that. The papa asked for some tobacco, but then he changed his mind for some reason. While Mr. Levy totaled up the bill, the papa asked if he could sit somewhere. His wooden leg was hurting him, it seemed. That got Mr. Levy's attention, and the papa said just one word, changed Mr. Levy's whole posture.

"Chickamauga," the papa said, pointing at his leg. I brought out a chair for him to sit.

Mr. Levy nodded and then pretended like he was finishing up the bill, but I knew he'd already done it. While he was doing it, the papa took a battered old leather purse out of his pocket and started counting his money. He was real slow, not like he was stupid, but more like if he counted slower he'd wind up with more money.

"You know what?" Mr. Levy said, like he'd just thought of it. "I made a flub. This is supposed to be a three, not a five! Nathaniel! Will you check this again for me? My brain must be gettin' old."

Well, I was surprised he asked me, but I did check it. And it was supposed to be a five, after all. But all I said was, "Yes, sir. It should be a three, all right."

"Nathaniel's my checker-upper," he said. The papa's face showed a visible look of relief.

"Oh," Mr. Levy said. "I included your tobacco in that. Is that okay?"

"Yes, sir," the papa said. "I surely thank'ee."

"Well, you've got a long trip," Mr. Levy said. "Nathaniel, whyn't you get some licorice for the kids."

The papa started to say something, like he didn't think it'd be right, but Mr. Levy just said, "Kids get free licorice and ginger snaps on Tuesdays. We've always done that. Right, Nathaniel?"

"Ever since I been here," I replied, because, after all, the papa had no way a knowing it was only my first day, see.

I helped load up the wagon and saw the family off. Then I went back in. "Sir," I started to ask him, but he stopped me.

"Nathaniel, sometimes you gotta put brotherhood ahead of profit."

I thought about that, and the more I thought, the better it sounded. "But, Mr. Levy," I asked him, "wasn't you a *Union* soldier?"

"I try not to make that common knowledge around here," he said.

"But if he was from the South—"

"Nathaniel, he was a man trying to give his family a better life. Yes, I was in the Union Army. I joined up to keep the Union together and because I hate slavery. But I didn't join up to hurt men like him . . . and every day I have to face up to that's just what I did. Well, I don't have to do it anymore, and if I can give him a helping hand, why, that's just what I'll do."

He stopped talking, and then he looked away from me. I went out and started moving some barrels around, and a few minutes later, he came out blowing his nose.

Anyhow, Mr. Levy set me to work right away on the first day as though I'd been with him all my life instead of with Tom Tryer. I thought I'd be sweepin' out the store and unloading barrels and sacks and such, and I did. Boy, did I ever! Mr. Levy also had me do something called inventory, which is where you go and count how much of each thing you have and how much you think you need, and you write it down. That way, you know how much you have to order from the folks who you buy the stuff from. There was all kinds of inventory to do since Mr. Levy sold everything under the sun, it seemed. He told me inventory was the most tiresome part of running a store, but also the most important. It didn't matter to me, because so long as I didn't have to wipe out spittoons, I figured anything was a step up.

Mr. Levy also kept something I didn't have to inventory at all, which he called a "consignment shelf." It actually weren't no shelf but a whole display case, but that's what he called it anyway. Sometimes people came in, like from the saloon, having lost all their money at the poker table or at Faro. They wanted Mr. Levy to loan them money in trade for which they'd give him their watch or gun or ring. Well, Mr. Levy explained in no uncertain words that he would never allow anyone to call him a money lender, so what he did was, he'd buy the stuff outright for a fair price instead of keeping it as a trade. Now, if they wanted to buy it back, say if they'd suddenly got lucky at the gaming table, why, he'd give it right back for the same amount he'd bought it for. But if someone came in and bought it first, well, that was that. That was the chance they took. But they didn't really lose nothing, because Mr. Levy'd sell it for more than he paid and split the profit with the original guy if he claimed it within sixty days. Seemed fair to me, though Jake later told me it was a whole lot more'n fair.

Jake himself bought something off the consignment shelf the first time he come in. See, the marshal's office was right next door, and Jake was having his first day same as me. Course, he had a lot less work to do.

"Well, young Nathaniel," he said and shook my hand. "Aaron, how are you?"

Mr. Levy, his first name was Aaron, see. He and Jake just started calling each other by their first name once they figured they were going to be friends.

"Jake, I have that Army Colt you need. And a good strong holster."

Jake nodded and took the holster from Mr. Levy. Mr. Levy had already filled up the little loops with extra bullets. Jake lifted his coat and hitched up the holster.

"Never thought I'd wear one a these again," Jake said. Mr. Levy held the Colt upside down and handed it to Jake. Even though it was empty, Jake opened the cylinder and checked it. Without saying nothing, Mr. Levy gave him a handful of bullets, and Jake loaded it up. Then he placed it in the holster.

"Feels heavier than I remember," Jake said with a small grin. "Aaron, have you got something smaller?"

Mr. Levy smiled. "I think I just might." He walked Jake over to the consignment shelf. "A fancy dude sold it to me a year ago. Lost his money in the casino. I guess he won't be coming back. Just off the stage from the East."

He lifted the glass display window and came up with a small black pistol with the butt curved almost like a Derringer. But it was a six-gun, all right.

"I've heard of these," Jake said, "But I've never seen one before. What do they call it again?"

"Double-action," Mr. Levy said. "It works, too; I've fired it. And cleaned it. It's only a thirty-two caliber, but you wouldn't be going for distance, would you? Anyway, the bigger calibers have too heavy a trigger pull and aren't as accurate."

I didn't know much about guns at the time, but even I knew I was seeing something worthwhile. I marveled as Jake pointed the empty gun and fired it. And here was the interesting thing: He didn't have to cock it first. He just pulled the trigger, and the gun cocked itself. What a invention! He could cock it if he wanted to, but why would he want to?

"Jake?" I asked him. "How come you need two guns? A feller who can shoot as good as you? And if you don't like 'em anyhow, why more'n one?"

Jake looked at Mr. Levy and then at me. "Those're good questions, Nate. They deserve a good answer. I don't like 'em, but if I'm to be a lawman, I have to go all the way and do it right. This little gun goes right here where no one can see it."

He lifted his topcoat and placed the gun in his trouser belt just behind his right hip. Then he closed his coat, straightened a little, and turned in a small circle. "Can you see it?" he asked me.

I couldn't, not even a tiny bit of it, and I told him so.

"Well, if a smart young fellow like you can't see it, then nobody else can, either."

"But what for?"

"Let me ask you a question, young Nathaniel. Let's say you don't like me, or just don't like lawmen. And you figure you're going to teach me a lesson. So one night, you . . . bushwhack? Yes, that's right, you bushwhack me and take my Colt away from me. How do you feel about that?"

I thought for a minute. "You mean, how do *I* feel about it, or how does the bushwhacker feel about it?"

"The bushwhacker."

"Well, pretty good, I guess."

"You'd say I'm in trouble, right?"

"Well, yeah."

"But, young Nathaniel, you got the drop on me. You've got a gun, and I don't. Or at least, that's what you think. So you relax. You might even turn your head for a second. And that'd be all I'd need. How will you feel when all of a sudden, you find out that maybe I *do* have a gun and it's pointing right at you?"

"Oh," I said. "Stupid, I guess."

He knocked on my head like it was somebody's bedroom door. It didn't hurt, though. "Gotta use that, young Nathaniel. Be prepared for every situation. A lawman has enough surprises in his life, doesn't need any more. But let's keep this between us, okay?"

"I'm sure Nathaniel will keep his word," Mr. Levy said.

"I appreciate that," Jake said. "And now, if it's all right with you, I'd like to borrow the young man for a little while. Nathaniel, would you mind giving me the fifty-cent tour of this sprawling metropolis?"

I guess he was talking about the town. But I didn't see why he needed a tour; all he had to do was look up the street one way and down the other, and that'd cover just about everything.

"There ain't a lot to see," I told him.

"Oh, but there is," he said. He nodded, and I fell into step with him.

"Just have him back by lunchtime," Mr. Levy called.

Jake nodded and waved back at him. "Settling in at the store okay?" he asked me.

"Yes, sir," I said. "Mr. Levy is a good man to work for."

"I imagined he would be," Jake agreed.

"What did you mean before, when you said there was a lot to see in town?"

"You tell me. What do *you* see?"

I was to get that a lot in the times to come. Jake never answered a question straight when I asked him one. He'd always ask me one right back. Funny thing was, it made it easier to understand when he finally did answer the question.

"Just a long dirt street with a bunch of shops and saloons on either side," I replied.

"Is that all?"

"Pretty much. Why? What do you see?"

"What I see, young Nathaniel, is my beat."

"Your what?"

"My beat. The place I'm sworn to protect. It's my job to get to know everyone who lives and works here, what they do, and when they do it. I'll make it easy for you," he added as we passed by Mr. Stout's bank. "When is this bank open for business?"

I read the sign on the door. "From nine until three," I said.

"All right. They open at nine, close at three, and maybe take another few hours to do all the day's accounts. So Mr. Stout and his employees go home around six. Now, what if I walk past there at nine at night and I see a light on inside?"

"I guess it could mean somebody done broke in."

"Yes. Or it could be a particularly busy time for Mr. Stout, say the first of the month when mortgages come due, and he's working late. It's important I know which, isn't it?"

"I guess so," I said. "I didn't think of that."

"When's the busiest time of the month at the saloon?"

"First and the middle of the month, when the miners and ranch hands get paid," I said. "That's what pays for the rest of the time, when there's hardly nobody a'tall."

"Well, now, it's important I know that, too," he told me. "When does the stage come to town?"

"Mondays and Fridays," I said.

"Then I'll be seeing strangers on Mondays and Fridays. I'll be busiest at the beginning and the middle of the month. But—"

He was cut off by the sound of a gunshot from the saloon.

"You'd best get back, Nathaniel."

But I didn't want to. What I wanted was to see Jake in action.

"I'll stick with you, if'n you don't mind," I said. "I'll stay outta your way, though."

"All right. Keep behind me."

There was another shot, the sound of glass breaking, followed by yet another with more glass breaking. So far, t'was nothing I ain't never heard before. Even from the street I could tell it was just some drunk shooting up the place.

"Does Ike have a gun?" Jake asked me as we trotted toward the saloon.

"What?" I shouted over another gunshot.

"The bartender. Does he have a gun?"

"Yeah," I said, lowering my voice as we reached the swinging door. "But he don't never use it. He can't shoot." He couldn't, either. I never saw nothing like it. Ike was right-handed, see, but he held the gun over to his left eye. Messed up his aim. Couldn't hit doodley-squat if he were up to his neck in it.

I thought Jake would just push his way on through the swinging doors, but he didn't. He stood off to the side and peered around first.

"Nathaniel," he whispered. "Take a quick peek. Be careful. Tell me what you see."

Well, they wasn't much. Ike was probably down under the bar and they was only a few customers that early in the day. They was hiding under the tables. The shooter was sitting at a table with his feet up, taking aim at the bottles on the bar.

"Ned Harper," I said. "He's drunk again."

"Is he a miner? A ranch hand?"

"Prospector," I said. "Only he don't find very much. Just enough for a bender, is all. He don't mean no harm."

Jake nodded and called through the door. "Say, Ned! Is that you?"

"Who wants to know?" Ned's gruff voice came back.

"Town marshal. You all right in there?"

"Well, I'll be go to hell," Ned replied, blasting another bottle. Of course, whether it were the bottle at which he was aiming, I had no idea. "Didn't know we had a new marshal yet. Come on in have a drink with me, Marshal."

"Well, I'd like to, Ned, but I get a little jumpy around a fellow shooting off a gun."

"Ain't no call to get jumpy, Marshal. I'm jes' celebratin'. Come on in. I ain't gonna shootcha."

"Well, I was more worried about my shooting you, Ned. I don't want to do that, and I don't think you want me to do that. Tell you what. Why don't you pay old Ike what you owe him, toss that six-shooter out my way, then you and I'll go and talk things over."

There was a moment of silence followed by another shot.

"I don't know as I can do that, Marshal. I think old Ike's pretty mad at me."

"Don't worry about it, Ned. Old Ike won't do a thing, will you, Ike?"

Silence.

"I said, will you, Ike?"

"I won't do nothin'," Ike's voice came grumpily from behind the bar.

"All right, Ned. I'm coming in. I won't have my gun out, so I'm counting on you as a man of your word."

"Jake," I whispered. "Jake, you gonna go in without your gun?"

Jake looked at me and winked. "Coming in, Ned," he called and stepped inside the bar. I dared to peek in behind him.

Jake walked right up to the table where Ned was sitting with his feet up. Ned looked like he always did after a month or so in the hills. His beard was all matted and stringy, and I guessed he probably didn't smell too good, neither.

"Hello, Ned," Jake said, and then he just as sweet as pie took the gun right out of Ned's big, dirty paw.

"Damn," Jake said. "A Colt .44 Model 1860! I haven't seen one of these in years! Where'd you get it?"

"Army of Northern Virginia, 'n later with Colonel Mosby," Ned said. "Served me damn well agin' them Yankees, I can tell you."

"Well, it sure is a beauty! But, Ned! Don't you ever clean this thing? Looks like you've been greasing wagon wheels with it!"

It was just then that Ike finally got himself over the bar and headed full steam toward Ned with his truncheon.

"Jake!" I shouted.

Jake didn't even look, just pushed Ned out of the way as fast as he could. Even so, Ike managed to slog a glancing blow on Ned's shoulder.

"Drop that," Jake said coldly.

"Who's gonna make me?" Ike replied just as coldly.

Moving even faster than during the fight with Earl Wilson, Jake grabbed Ike's wrist, the one holding the club, and twisted. Ike screamed in pain and dropped the stick.

"Don't you ever," Jake said in a low, scary voice, "ever touch a man who is in my custody."

"Goddamn it all!" shouted Ike. "Who's gonna pay for them bottles?"

Jake shrugged. "Well, Ned was going to. That was before you attacked an unarmed man in police custody and threatened an officer of the law."

" 'S all right, Marshal," said Ned, who was beginning to belch a little dangerously. "I done busted 'em up; I'll pay fer'm."

"What's the damage?" Jake asked.

"Eleven dollars and forty-two cent."

Ned reached into his pocket and took out a greasy wad of bills and some coins. "There y'are, my good man. Twelve dollars. Keep the change."

"All right?" Jake asked Ike.

Ike grunted. "Just get him outta here."

"Ned," Jake said. "Why don't we go across to my office. You look like you could use a few days' rest."

"Why that's right neighborly of you, Marshal. I guess I did disturb the peace just a bit, didn't I?"

"I'm afraid so," Jake said.

"Tell you what," Ned said with a serious expression. "You jes' let me upchuck a bit, and we'll be right on our way."

"That's another five dollars, goddamn it!" Ike shouted.

3

WE HALF-CARRIED OLD Ned out to the privy, where he calmly upchucked to his heart's content. Then we brought him over to Jake's office, where he quietly thanked us for our help, staggered into an open cell, and collapsed into a ferocious sleep, snoring loud enough to like take the roof off.

I worked far into the night that first workday. Not because Mr. Levy made me but because I wanted to. It seemed to me there was a lot more to running a business than I thought there was, and I wanted to finish up that damned inventory so's I could help Mr. Levy with customers during the day. It turned out I liked waiting on customers. There was something about trading a pleasant good day and getting someone exactly what they wanted and sending them away happy that agreed with me. It was sure as hell better than being something you just stepped around, like at the saloon.

Anyhow, Mr. Levy finally kicked me out at around ten

o'clock, insisting I get myself a good dinner and a decent night's sleep.

"Dinner's on me," he said, flipping me a fifty-cent piece. "You earned it. I'm glad you're in my employ, Nathaniel."

Well, no one ever said that to me before, and for some stupid reason my lip started to tremble and I couldn't trust myself to say nothing back to him, so I just nodded and went out.

I was on my way back to my room, looking forward to my first night's sleep in a real bed. I'd forgotten all about it because I'd been so busy all day. I was hungry, too, and I was hoping the kitchen would still be open.

But as I passed by Jake's office, I saw that the light was still on, so I stopped in.

"Well, hello, Nate," Jake said. It was getting a little confusing. I wasn't used to anybody being happy to see me or even caring if I was alive one way or another.

"Our guest just woke up," he said, nodding toward the cell, where various unpleasant sounds of life were coming from old Ned.

"Coffee . . ." Ned croaked. Jake poured him a cup from the old kettle left by the last marshal.

"Thankee," Ned muttered, greedily slugging it down. How he managed not to burn the hell out of his throat was beyond me. He held out the cup, and Jake refilled it. Ned drank more slowly this time.

"Never get used to good coffee," Ned grunted. "Beats that chicory 'n acorn slop we got durin' the war."

"How do you feel, Ned?"

"Hell of a lot better'n I prob'ly look," he said. "How you doin' there, kid," he said to me. "This young fella yer deputy?" he asked Jake without waiting for me to answer.

"Young Nate helps me out from time to time," Jake said. "Tell me, Ned. You said this morning that you were celebrating. What were you celebrating?"

Ned looked at the open door and then at Jake. I took the hint and closed it. He motioned us both closer to him, which wasn't much of a treat, considering the various odors coming off him.

He looked around again and said in a low whisper, "I were up in Pima Canyon," he said.

"And?" Jake prompted him.

"I done found it! The biggest garldarned silver strike this side a Casa Grande. Bigger'n 'at sumbitch Wilson's! Bigger'n th' one in Tombstone, I'll betcha!"

"Well, that's great, Ned," Jake said. Jake had this slight smile on his face, the old mustache twitch, that tipped me that maybe he thought old Ned had a good imagination.

"Goddamn it, I ain't sportin'!" Ned shouted. Then he put his hand over his mouth to shut himself up. He reached into his pocket and took out a little leather bag tied with a string. He undid the string and emptied it on the floor.

"What's that look like to you?" he demanded. "A horse turd?"

Jake picked some of it up and sifted it through his fingers. "I apologize, Ned. You're quite right. Congratulations are in order."

"Well, no, they ain't," he said miserably, shaking his head. "I cain't work the goddamn claim. Not for a coupla months, anyhow. I ain't got the scratch for new supplies and provisions."

"You just paid Ike Hawkins twelve dollars for the privilege of shooting some bottles over his bar," Jake reminded him.

"I did? Damn whiskey! That leaves me a dollar'n a half. Shoot! By the time I make enough for supplies, somebody else'll find it and jump it. Prob'ly a Wilson!"

"You sure it's a strike?" Jake asked.

"Yer abso-god-damn tootin'!" Ned said. "I been prospectin' almost fifteen year, since end a the damn war. I think I know my bidness by now. Who you think found that coyote Wilson's strike?"

"*You* did?" I couldn't believe it. That strike had made Wilson one of the richest men in the territory.

"What the hell you think Wilson knows about prospectin'? He's a damn cattleman! An' he ain't even much good at that!"

"Tell us about it, Ned," Jake urged him.

Ned proceeded to unfold the whole dirty story. He come out here right after the war, having heard somewhere that Arizona was nothing but one big silver mine, just under the ground and waiting to be tapped. There were stories like that making the rounds of both armies, but they caught on especially among the Johnny Rebs, who knew they'd be going home to precious little as it became clear the war was all but lost.

Old Ned's father had been a plantation overseer before the war, a job that Ned would have learned and then inherited, but the freeing of the slaves changed all that. There was nothing for him to go back to. So, after the surrender, he headed west, spending a year among prospectors and picking up whatever knowledge he could from whoever was willing to teach him. By the time he reached town, he could pass himself off as a man of experience.

It was at the saloon that he met Tom Tryer and Alvin Wilson. There had been a few small strikes in the nearby hills, but nothing to holler about. He struck a deal with Tryer and Wilson; they'd back him, and he'd do all the work in exchange for a full one-third interest.

Well, Ned was as good as his word. The strike he found in the hills just outside town was big—big enough to make all of them rich.

"I shoulda seen it comin'," he said to us, although his eyes were looking back to years ago. "They paid me what they thought was enough for my time and cut me right out. I called 'em lowdown scum-suckin' rattlesnakes, but they told me I didn't have nothin' in writing."

"What did you do?" I asked.

"Well, what could I do? They was right. I coulda took 'em to court, but what could I prove?"

"He's right," Jake said. "It would have been his word against theirs."

"Well, I got 'em this time, Marshal," Ned said. "This time, it's *my* strike, and you c'n swear to it for me. I just wish I didn't hafta wait so goddamn long to work it."

"How much do you need to work it?" I asked, just out of curiosity.

Ned rubbed his scraggly beard and came away with something he flicked away between his fingers. "Oh," he began, looking at the ceiling as he figured it out, "I guess about eighty or ninety dollars, plus a new mule. I got a couple a good Pima Injun fellas wanna help me out, 'n they said they'll work agin' the first coupla batches a silver we pull outta there.

Then he added, for no reason I could see, "I'm dry when I work. I on'y get drunk in town."

Jake said, "I'd like to help you out, Ned. I really would.

But if it got out that I did, my word on your claim would be useless."

"I guess we cain't have that, Marshal," Ned agreed. "But yer a good egg, all right, for sayin' so."

My heart suddenly leapt into my mouth. I had an idea, and before I could even consider it, I said, "I'll give you the money, Ned. In exchange for one-third interest in your mine."

Ned exploded into a huge cough-laugh that like to make me sick. "You will!" he said finally. *"You* will?"

"I got one hundred and thirty-seven dollars in Mr. Stout's bank," I said. I'd been putting away nickels and dimes into my savings ever since I could remember. Not that I ever made much money, but what little I did make, I didn't need to spend on anything, and there was no other safe place to put it. I figured someday I'd have a use for it, even if it was to just buy a horse and get out of town. But there was never anything that called to me before. Until now.

"Yeah," I said. "I will."

Old Ned cackled with glee and slapped me on the back. It damn well hurt, too. "Well, ain't you the young game 'un," he shouted, then hushed himself. "You're gonna be the youngest rich sumbitch inna whole territory!"

I felt myself flush, but with what, I couldn't tell. Embarrassment? Fear? Excitement? Maybe all those things?

Jake turned to me. "Are you sure you want to do this, Nathaniel? It's not a sure thing. You could lose all of your money, and I know how hard you worked for it."

To tell the truth, I *wasn't* sure I wanted to do it. I was only sure that I didn't want to let an opportunity pass me by. You grow up in a saloon, and you find out how few of them come along.

"I may turn out to be sorry I did it," I said to Jake. "But I'll be a lot sorrier if I didn't."

"Good enough," Jake said. "Let's write this up, you two sign, and I'll witness it. We'll keep it here, where it'll be safe. Ned, Nate says his end is one-third. That all right with you?"

"Jake with me," he replied. "Oh, not to make light a yer Christian name there, Marshal."

Jake nodded and said, "Thirty-three and a third percent to you, Nate. Is that all right with you?"

"No," I said.

"Why the hell not!" roared Ned. "I mean, if you want a little more, okay, but—"

"That's not what I mean," I said. "I'll take the one-third. Sort of. I want twenty-three and a third percent. The other ten percent goes to—"

"Goes to whom?" Jake asked, and I thought I saw the mustache twitch again.

I took a deep breath and wondered if I was being a stupe. "Goes to . . . Rebecca Levy," I said in a rush.

"Rebecca Levy," Jake said, writing it down. He stopped and turned to me. "My, my," Jake said. "Rebecca is an awfully lucky girl, and she doesn't even know it."

Mr. Levy's sabbath was on Saturday, but he worked most of the day, anyhow. There wasn't no church for his faith anywhere near our end of the territory, so he took off a few hours in the morning for private worship with his family and then came in to work. He said he figured the Lord ought to be a reasonable enough fellow to understand the situation.

He insisted that I take Sundays off, even though I never been in a church in my whole life and had no real interest in starting now. He told me that might change someday, and I still ought to have the day off just for myself.

Well, I never had a day off in my life, and if it hadn't been for the mine, I wouldn't of known what-all to do with myself. On my first Sunday off, I hitched a ride with Jake over to the mine just to look in on things.

Pima Canyon was about ten or twelve miles out of town, and it was one of those days right after the rainy season that the whole desert just seems to come alive. We get a few months of the devil's own rain every year, and everything just seems to close up and disappear. But about six and a half seconds after the rain stops, it's like everything in nature just calls out to its friends and says, "Come on out! It's a fine day after all!" The desert rats and ring-tailed deer and rattlesnakes and coyotes and Gila monsters all seem to get up and stretch and yawn and then run wild with glee that the damn rain is finally over. Plants and flowers that wasn't there yesterday just spring up before your very eyes. It kind of makes you forget how empty and sad the scorching desert can make you feel a few months later. Or how much you might agree with General Sherman, who said, "We went to war with Mexico for Arizona—we ought to go war again to make them take it back!"

I didn't know beans about silver mining . . . or any other type of mining, for that matter. I figured you took a pan and squatted next to a stream, and if a rattler didn't bite you in the butt, you came away with enough dust to cash in at the assayer's and then went to the saloon to get drunk and go upstairs with one a the girls. Then you came downstairs, drank some more whiskey, picked a fight, and got thrown out into the street and wound up facedown in a puddle.

Either that, or you took a pick and shovel and went down into the bottom of a mountain, banged the crap out of a few rocks, and took them into town and went into the saloon and still wound up facedown in the same puddle.

Well, it turned out a bit different than all that. Silver ain't like gold, which I knew, but I didn't know why.

"With yer gold, see," Ned explained, "all ya gotta do is separate it from the rock, filter it out somehow. Them ancient fellas, the ones in Araby someplace . . . or was it the Greeks . . . cain't keep them damn ferners straight nohow, they usedta strain it through a sheepskin. That's where ya got that old Golden Fleece story I wunst heard when I were a boy."

We were standing over a pit of burning mesquite; that is, we were standing near it. One of Ned's Pima Injuns, who he called Fred because he couldn't pronounce his real name, kept adding more and more mesquite to the fire. It was so hot I couldn't stand being within ten feet of it.

"That's a hot fire you've got, Ned," Jake pointed out, stepping back.

"Well, hell, yeah! It's gotta be hot. See, with your silver, it don't wanna separate from the rest a the rock . . . like it's a favorite gal or some such. It's all mixed in. So you burn a buncha mesquite into charcoal. How we doin' there, Fred?" he asked the Injun, slapping him on the back.

Fred nodded and placed a big rock on a pan with holes in it over the fire, kind of like a blacksmith making horseshoes. In a few minutes, the rock began to melt.

"I ain't sure how it works, 'cause it's some kinda chemical foolishness I ain't had enough schoolin' to figure, but the rocks burn, see. All the crap on it that ain't silver, well that gits attracted to the crap burnin' off the mesquite, an' it just shoots up to meet it and say hidy. Everything what you got left in the pan, why, that's your silver!"

Fred took the pan off the fire and dunked it into a bucket of water. It made a hiss loud enough to think the silver itself was complaining.

Ned took a drink from his canteen. "Water," he said. "I told ya I'm dry when I work."

Fred showed us the results of his work, maybe a dozen tiny bits of a dull metal. He looked at us the way a cook might to see if you liked your dinner.

Ned stuck a big, gloved paw into the cooled pan and picked up one of the pieces. "There it is, by God! The best confounded silver in all Arizona! Y' c'n almost squeeze it in your fingers! Jus' like the Tombstone Lode! Better, I'll betcha!"

"Hold on there a minute," I said. "You mean, outta that big rock, all you got was a couple squat-doodle little pieces?"

Ned looked at me, a little sad and a little peeved at the same time. "What'd you think it'd be? Why inna huckleberry hell you think you need hunnerds a men to work a mine? Just be glad it ain't gold, son. You find a ton a ore, all ya git is less'n a half ounce a gold! Now, you jus' go on about yore business and leave the minin' to me an' m' boys. You'll get yore grubstake back and more'n y'ever dreamed of besides. Now, go on! We got work t'do, an' no time to fiddle-fart around! Go on, now."

"I guess I shouldn't a said that," I told Jake as we headed back toward town.

Jake shrugged. "You didn't know. And I'm sure he meant nothing by it. But Ned's been working hard all week. It's a tough job for just three men. They've got a lot of hard labor ahead of them."

"I hope they'll be all right up there," I said. "There's plenty of claim jumpers around here."

"I'll look in on them from time to time," Jake assured me. "Don't worry, son. I'll see to it that your investment is secure."

Well, I didn't feel real secure. Seeing how much work it took just for a few little scraps of silver made me feel a bit downhearted. It would take months and months before any real money came out of the mine. And even then, that money couldn't go into my pocket. Ned would have to hire more men and buy better equipment. And even that would make things worse. Right now, the mine was a secret. But sooner or later, someone—or everyone— would catch on. Jake alone couldn't protect the mine and do his marshal's job at the same time. Tom Tryer and the Wilsons would start sniffing around, too.

Jake was looking sideways at me. He nodded his head. "It's not easy being a silver tycoon, is it?"

4

TOM TRYER'S ESTABLISHMENT took up two buildings put together. The saloon and gambling hall was one building, and anybody was welcome to just drop on in—anybody with money on them, that is.

The second building you couldn't get into except through the gambling hall, and to do that you had to pass muster with Tom Tryer or one a his big apes who didn't do much except look nasty and wait for you to do something that'd give 'em an excuse to throw you out on your ear. The other building was a lot different. I used to help out in there, sweeping and mopping and changing the linen. That was Miss Flora's establishment. Actually, it was Tom Tryer's *and* Miss Flora's establishment. They split the business somehow, but I'm not sure who got what share or how much it was.

Miss Flora was a fine, handsome lady from somewhere back East, and she was in charge of all the girls. The saloon and gambling hall could be pretty rough when all the fellows were in town on payday, but never Miss

Flora's. It was all decorated with fancy furniture and rich, brocaded curtains, like what I figured a big-city hotel would be. Everybody had to behave in Miss Flora's, or the apes showed them the door right quick.

First of all, you couldn't even get into Miss Flora's without you took a bath first. But that was okay, they had baths available, for a price. I oughta know, I drew enough of 'em.

Next, you couldn't be drunk. If you was drunk, you caused a problem, and Miss Flora did not want problems. She liked her operation to run smooth.

Also, you couldn't use bad language, because Miss Flora said bad language led to bad behavior, and besides, there was ladies present. Of course, I'd heard Miss Flora use bad language herself on occasion, but that didn't have nothing to do with anyone else using it, I guessed.

Last of all, and this was something she had the apes make damned sure of, no guns were allowed inside. Of course, she always had a derringer handy, but she owned the place. You took off your gun at the door, and it was kept safe for you—also for a small price.

Miss Flora liked to say that she was in the business of making little boys' dreams come true. And I guess she was pretty good at it. It was said her end of the operation was worth more than Tom Tryer's, and I believed it. The truth was, I believed everything she said, because I liked her. She was one of those women who looked you square in the eye and never blinked. And she was always nice to me. I worked like hell for her, but she always said thank you and you're a good boy, Nate, and never once threw a towel at my ear.

She was as pretty as any of the two dozen girls who worked for her, although a bit older, but she ran the place, and that was all. There was only one fellow who she disappeared with, and that was Alvin Wilson. I didn't know why she'd let an old coot like that have his way with her, but she never asked me what I thought.

That was also why the Wilson boys were able to get around some of her strict house rules. Anybody did half the things they did would have been up to his neck in ape fists and kicks.

What would happen was they'd cause some trouble—they never took off their guns, even for her—shoot up the place or get drunk or hurt one of the girls, and the apes would run to her and tell her about it. Then she'd come down and say go on, boys, behave or get out, and they'd say, sorry Flora, won't happen again. But it always did.

Well, when we got back into town, Tom Tryer met Jake's wagon. Tom was a tall, slender fellow who it was said had got his grubstake as a card sharp on the Mississippi riverboats. He always dressed like a dude with lots of frills and ruffles, and he had a long, thin mustache that he always kept carefully waxed. He spoke with a Southern drawl that was so thick I figured it had to be fake, but of course I never called him on it. Still, he liked to keep up the appearance of a Mississippi gambling swell, and I guess it was a lot easier for people to believe him.

Anyhow, Tom called us over and was about to say something when he took one look at Jake and shut up quick. I saw Jake's eyes get all narrow and then I looked over at Tom who appeared scared to death.

Jake saw me staring at him and Tom Tryer and gave the kind of cough people do when they want to change the subject, though we wasn't talking about nothing to begin with.

"Who's that gentleman?" he asked me.

"Why, that's Tom Tryer."

"Oh," he said, like he just discovered the answer to something he'd been trying to figure out all day long. "Mr. Tryer," he said. "I'm Marshal Murchison. How can I be of assistance?"

Tom sort of shook and blinked and licked his lips a few times and said, "Oh, Marshal, nice to meet you. We need your help over to Miss Flora's."

"Lead the way," Jake said.

"Uh, Tom," I said. He turned to me, and before he could say anything, I went on real quick. "Tom, I tried to see you to say good-bye and good luck before I went to work for Mr. Levy, but Ike just tol' me to get out, so I didn't get the chance, so's I'm saying it now. Thank you, Tom, you been real kindly toward me, and if there's ever anything I can do for you to return the favor, why, you just say so, and I'll come runnin'. "

I was almost out of breath when I finished. I'd never said so much to Tom in my life, and if Jake hadn't been there, he probably would have considered it impudence.

"This young man was obviously well brought up," Jake said. "Maybe you had something to do with that."

Tom blinked a few more times and gave me a quick smile, the kind someone does because they have to, so it only lasts a second.

"That's quite all right, Nate," he said quickly. "You was a good worker."

"Well, that's settled," Jake said cheerfully. "Now, what's going on, *Tom?*" I don't know why he said Tom's name so hard, but my former boss looked like he'd been stung by a bee.

"Uh, there's trouble at Miss Flora's. The Wilson brothers."

"That's all right, I'll see to it," Jake said.

We fell into step beside Tom. He looked over at me like I was something on the bottom of his shoe.

"Nathaniel is assisting me today," Jake said. "You don't have a problem with that, do you, *Tom?*"

Tom mumbled something, and didn't say nothing else until we got inside to Miss Flora's. Miss Flora took one look at Jake and was smitten right away, you could tell that if you was blind or drunk. She got up real quick and sort of smoothed her dress over her bosom the way girls do when a fellow looks good to them.

She put out her hand for him to shake. "Marshal Murchison, is it? I'm Flora Jenks," she said.

"Miss Jenks," Jake replied, touching his hat. It was funny, but when he did that, I saw something right inside my head. It was like I could read Jake's mind. He was thinking, *Well, you sure are pretty and seem darn smart, but falling for you would be a mistake, so we'll just keep it friendly.* Don't ask me how I knew that, but I did.

"How may I be of assistance, Miss Jenks?"

"Oh, it's those confounded Wilson boys again!"

"All of them?" Jake asked.

"No, just Bob and Buck. They've got Janie and Edna up there, and they're not keeping their promise."

"What promise?"

Flora looked over at me, as if my being there made her too shy to talk about it. I couldn't figure that one; I damn near grew up in her establishment, after all. There wasn't nothin' I hadn't seen, although I didn't seem too much the worse for it.

But just to be polite to Miss Flora, I put my hands over my ears.

"Oh, Nate," Miss Flora said with a smile, "you always were too smart for your own good." She turned to Jake. "Whips," I saw her whisper.

"It got out of hand, did it?" Jake replied. "All right, lead the way."

It was Miss Flora's own idea that each of the ten rooms be made to look like someplace that wasn't in Arizona. One room might be made up to look like a fancy lady's parlor. Another was called the Haystack Room, which had a farm scene painted on the wall and a real haystack in it. And there was another one made to look like a dungeon, with the walls made up like stone. That was where the Wilsons liked to go most of all.

Well, when we got into the Dungeon Room, Janie and Edna was crying in a corner, and the Wilson boys was laughing and slugging from a bottle of whiskey. Janie and Edna were both real young, not much older'n me, but they'd been around for awhile. Buck Wilson was sweet on Janie, but Janie wouldn't have nothing to do with him beyond business arrangements.

Anyhow, Janie had a couple a whip marks on her. They wasn't bleeding, but they was swollen. I'd been around Miss Flora's often enough to know that fellas who like whips usually don't mean no harm by it. Whether they're givin' or receivin', they only do it so nobody gets hurt. I can think of much more pleasant ways to spend time with a pretty girl, but what other people do ain't up to me.

"Goddamn, Flora," Buck said with a belch, "you didn't have to go an' call the law! We'se jus' havin' some fun, is all."

"You call this fun?" Janie demanded, pointing to a big welt on her stomach.

Jake beckoned to the girls, who gave Buck and Bob a wide berth as they headed to the door.

"Two questions," Jake said to them. "You don't have to say anything. Just nod yes, or shake your head no. First, were you forced to do anything for which you did not previously agree or were not going to be paid?"

The girls looked to Flora for approval and then nodded fearfully.

"Next," Jake said, "did you try to leave the room, and if so, were you forcibly prevented from leaving?"

Again the girls nodded. "Thank you, ladies," Jake said, touching the brim of his hat. "You may go and see to yourselves."

He nodded to Miss Flora, who ushered the girls out of the room. He then noticed that Tom Tryer was peeking into the room from the outside.

"That'll be all, *Tom,*" he said. "Thank you for your help."

Tom beat it out of there quick.

"Gentlemen," he said to Buck and Bob, "you are under arrest."

"What the hell fer?" shouted Bob Wilson.

"Oh, let's see now," Jake said, as if he was thinking it up as he went along. "Assault. Battery. Public drunkenness. Unlawful imprisonment. The judge'll be especially interested in that last one."

I tapped Jake on the shoulder. "Not now, Nathaniel," he said.

"What's that little spittoon-washer doin' in here?" Buck demanded.

"Shut up," Jake said.

I tapped him on the shoulder again. He turned to me and I beckoned him closer. He widened his eyes as if to say, *What is it?*

"The judge," I whispered.

"What about him?"

"He owns ten percent of Wilson's mine," I whispered again.

"Why am I not surprised?" Jake replied. Then he smiled and patted my shoulder. "Thank you, Nathaniel. You're becoming rather indispensable."

"Okay, boys," he said. "Here's what we're going to do. You're each fined twenty dollars and forbidden to enter this establishment again until I see fit to allow you entrance."

"You cain't do that!" Bob protested.

"I am doing it."

"Our paw ain't gonna like this!" Buck threatened.

"Really?" Jake replied. He stood with his hand on his hip. "This is me giving a damn." He stood stock-still. "This is me not giving a damn. Can you tell the difference?"

I thought that was pretty funny, but I didn't laugh.

"Now, hand over your fines."

Bob picked up his pants and dug into his pockets. "I only got twelve dollars left."

"I only got sixteen and some," Buck said.

"That'll do for now," Jake said, snatching it out of their fists. "You pay me the rest tomorrow, or it's one night in jail for each dollar you owe."

"We'll get you for this," Buck said in a low voice.

"I'm sorry," Jake said. "I wasn't paying attention. What was that you just said?"

"You heard me," Buck said in the same voice. "Me and my broth—"

Buck never did finish what he was saying, because Jake's fist come from out of nowhere, it seemed like, and next thing Buck was on the floor, out colder'n Ned Harper after a two-day drunk.

Jake gave a little stare at Bob, same as saying, *You want a nap, too?* Bob just took a step backward.

"When he wakes up," Jake said in a reasonable tone, "please be so good as to tell him that I don't take kindly to threats. You'll do that, won't you?"

"Yes, sir, Marshal. I'll do that all right."

"Well, now," said Jake. "You Wilson boys can be quite agreeable when you put your minds to it. Thank you, Bob. And don't forget the rest of that fine. Come along, young Nathaniel. I haven't had Sunday dinner yet, and I'm beginning to feel like a heathen."

Jake invited me to dine with him back at the hotel, which was no hardship at all, as anyone who ever et a steak at Zeb Stanton's could tell you. In the middle of dinner I couldn't hold out no more and came out with a question that'd been bothering me.

"It's none a my business, Jake," I began, "but I gotta ask you. Where d'you know Tom Tryer from?" I asked in a low voice so's nobody else could hear.

"You're right," he said. "It is none of your business." He gave out a quick laugh. "I don't mean it that way, Nathaniel. The way I figure things, plenty of men come west to leave one life behind and start afresh. I do believe that many years from now, some of the men who'll be most admired for settling this land will be fellows who left the East one step ahead of either the law or the bill collector."

"So you do know him, then," I said.

"I may not think much of the man," Jake said, "but I owe him the common decency of letting him be. As long as he obeys the law here in town, I have no quarrel with him. But his story is not mine to tell."

Well, my eyebrows kind of flew up in the way they do when I get really interested.

"Maybe someday," Jake said. "But not now. Save room for some pie, Nathaniel."

5

IT WAS KIND of funny, but even though I worked six long days a week for her father, I was seeing less and less of Rebecca. She was pretty busy with school and helping her ma, but even so, I thought since the store was right next to her house, I'd a seen her once in a while. After a few weeks it occurred to me that maybe she didn't want to see me. I got the hint when I saw her walking home from the schoolhouse with Beth Wilkins and Ashley Stout, and I said hidy but she acted like she didn't hear me. She never used to do that before I came to work for her pa. Even though the other girls acted like I was dirt under their toes, she was always friendly. So I couldn't understand it. Finally, I caught up with her one day when she was walking home alone.

"Oh, hello, Nate," she said, like it cost her something.

"Well, hello, Becky! It's sure been awhile! Where ya been?"

"I've been busy."

"Oh, what with?"

"Well, school, for one. We older kids have to memorize everybody who signed the Declaration of Independence . . . at least one from each state. Miz Thomas says maybe someday Arizona will be a state, too, so we should know all about it."

"One from each state?" I asked.

"Yes, and I keep getting them mixed up."

"Hmmm," I said, thinking for a minute. "New Hampshire, Josiah Bartlett. Massachusetts, John Adams. Connecticut, Roger Sherman. Rhode Island, Stephen Hopkins. New York, Lewis Morris. New Jersey, John Withersp—"

"Nathaniel!" she shouted at me.

"What? I read it in a book once."

"You just think you're the smartest kid alive, don't you? And you haven't ever set foot in the schoolhouse! It's not fair!"

"Hold on!" I argued. "I never said I was smarter than anybody else."

"But you are, darn it!"

Damn, she was pretty!

"Becky—" I began, but she cut me off.

"It's not fair," she said again. "I work so hard!" Her eyes got a little wet and all of a sudden I felt really strange, like I wanted to hug her or go beat somebody up if she asked me to.

"I just can't get it! I try to read, and the words look all funny! Like they're in another language. Everybody laughs at me, even my friends, even though they say they're sorry later, and Miz Thomas keeps telling me I'm not trying hard enough. But I am! I try harder than everybody else! Sometimes I stay up all night trying." She looked at me like it were my fault. "And you . . . you spent your whole life in that . . . that *place,* and you can read and remember better'n anyone, Miz Thomas even. Papa comes home for dinner every night and the first thing he says is, 'That Nathaniel's a wizard! How'd I ever run the store without him?' It's not fair!"

"Look," I said, feeling bad because I was proud knowing her pa thought so highly of me. "I'll help you. I know I can."

"*You'll* help *me?* Oh, that'll make me right popular when that gets out!"

I felt like Jake's right fist had just sunk into my stomach.

"What do you mean by that?" I said, my voice shaking.

She put her hand to her mouth. "Oh, my, Nate, I didn't mean—"

"Who thinks who's better'n who now?" I said hotly. "I grew up in a saloon, so you're better'n me? Well, you're still the one who can't read."

She looked like I'd just slapped her in the face. She turned away fast, but I took her arm.

"I'm sorry," I said. "I had no call to say that."

"Will you let go my arm?" she said coolly.

"I'll get you to read," I said.

"No, thank you."

"I'll get you to read," I repeated. "You don't have to tell no one. You can say your ma helped you."

I thought I saw the beginnings of a grin on her lips. "I'd never do that."

"Well, you can."

I picked up a stick and drew my name in the dirt. "What's that say?" I asked her.

"I don't know," she said. "Nate, I have to go—"

I thought for a second. I noticed that she narrowed her

eyes and seemed to be straining to read the big letters in the dirt. Something was wrong, way wrong. Becky was no imbecile. How could she not read my name, something as simple as N-A-T-E?

"Becky? Don't get mad at me, 'cause I ain't makin' fun of you. Do you need specs?"

"No," she said, choking a little. "Ma thought of that. She took me to see Doc Hayes when I was little, and then again a few years later. I can see fine."

"Wait here," I said. I walked off twenty paces and held up two fingers. "How many fingers am I holding up?"

"Two," she said.

"And now?"

"Four."

I walked back toward her. "Well, it ain't your eyesight, then. Damn! Sorry. What could it—Becky! I got a idea." I pointed to my name in the dirt and handed her the stick.

"You want me to give you the switch?" she said. "Because I will."

I thought of the Wilson brothers a few weeks before. "Another time," I replied, Jake-style. "No, what I want you to do is copy what you see in the dirt there. Right under what I wrote."

"That's stupid!"

"Just do it, anyhow," I ordered her. I thought it would take a long time, but she made a few quick scratches with the stick and . . . and I didn't know what in *the* hell I was looking at.

"Becky?" I said in a high, funny voice I could do nothing about. "Draw me a N."

"There."

Well, it sure in the hell didn't look like no N. "Is that what a N always looks like to you?"

"Well, yeah! What's an N *supposed* to look like?"

"Not like that," I said. "Like this."

"That's what I did!"

"Becky," I said as soft as I could, "no it weren't. I think your eyes turn letters upside down and back to front."

She put her hand to her mouth as if I'd just told her she had consumption.

"It ain't nothin bad," I said quickly. "Really it ain't. They's a feller in London, or one a them Europes—that feller you had me read at your house, I done heard he had the same thing wrong with him."

"Shakespeare?" she said like she didn't believe me, and she shouldn't have, because I was lying like a wrangler at a campfire bragging about his horse.

"Yes, ma'am," I said. "The very fellow. He got over it, too. Well, he didn't get over it, but his ma and them taught him what letters he was lookin' at was supposed to be which. Well, if a Englishman could do it, why not you?"

She got this look on her face, the kind of look if she was doing it for me I'd be happy for the rest of my life, like she wanted to cry but was happy at the same time.

"You think I can? You *really* think I can?"

"I'll help you. All I can, every free minute."

"Oh, Nate! I'd like that! I really would!" Like she weren't thinking about it, she gave me a quick kiss on the cheek and ran home.

I had trouble sleeping that night. Lots of trouble. But not the kind of trouble I could complain about to anybody, not even Jake. That was starting to happen plenty. In the few months I'd been working for Mr. Levy, things were happening inside me. It was like what I said before about the desert right after the rains. Maybe it was because I was eating better and sleeping better and doing heavy work, but I was starting to get taller and stronger. One day, I just looked down and saw my pants was above my ankles. I pointed it out to Mr. Levy who laughed and slapped me on the back and had me grab a new pair of pants.

I took a pair of those trousers we got in from San Francisco, the ones that miners seemed to like so much, made by Mr. Levi Strauss. It was my own secret joke, see. I couldn't tell nobody about the mine, but only miners wore Mr. Strauss's pants at the time, ranchers preferring corduroys and wool.

Anyhow, I was in the back of the store, changing into my new pants. I was having trouble buttoning them up, which was somehow embarrassing, even though no one saw me. That was starting to happen to me a lot, even when I wasn't inspired by thoughts of things I shouldn't of been thinking about Rebecca or for some reason Janie or Edna and even Miss Flora.

Anyhow, just as I was tucking in my shirttail, somebody come running into the store looking for Jake. I saw it was Fred, the Pima Injun working for Ned. I heard Mr. Levy direct him to Jake's office next door. Well, we wasn't real busy, so I ambled over to Jake's after Mr. Levy said I could take me a break.

Jake nodded for me to come in and then motioned for me to close the door. Which I did.

"Tell him, Fred," Jake said. He saw that Fred was all dry and gave him his canteen. Fred slugged away at it until it was almost empty.

"Claim-jumpers," Fred said raggedly. "We was just doing our work when Whitetail stops and puts his ear on the ground. 'Horses, maybe six or eight of 'em,' he says.

'They're headed up here 'n *fast.*' Well, Ned didn't waste no time sending me here for help."

"Did you see them?" Jake asked.

"Not close," Fred replied.

"Was it the Wilsons?" I asked him.

"Didn't look like no Wilsons."

"It wouldn't be," Jake told me. "If they just go in and grab it by force, it won't be legal. Instead, they get some hired guns to do their dirty work. Then the mine stays deserted, and they can just go in and grab it, because it doesn't belong to anybody anymore."

"Well, some of it belongs to *me,*" I said, feeling myself getting all red.

"Yes, but they don't know that."

"How'd they find it?" I asked him.

"It was bound to come out, Nathaniel. Maybe Ike told them he saw Ned celebrating, and they asked, 'Celebrating what?' and then put two and two together."

"Well, damn it, let's go," I said.

"Hold on there, Nate. You're not going anywhere. It's too dangerous. I'm not leaving Rebecca a widow before she even gets married."

"Damn it, it's my mine, too," I insisted. "I have the . . . the legal right to protect my own, don't I?"

He went to the gun rack and picked up a Winchester. "Ever used one of these before?"

I pointed to the barrel. "Bullet comes outta this end, don't it?"

Jake sighed and rolled his eyes. "Stick to me like glue," he said.

We could hear gunfire echoing off the canyons long before we reached the mine. It was occasional fire, like neither side could get a clear shot.

"Is there some high ground opposite the mine?" Jake asked Fred.

"Over that way," Fred said.

"I'm surprised he held out this long," Jake said.

"Well, before they come up here, Ned he had us bring as much water and provisions inside the mine as we could."

"That was smart," Jake nodded.

"Ned he were a good soldier wunst."

We had a commanding view of the action from where we sat. I counted eight men huddling behind rocks and slopes near the mine entrance. Ned and Whitetail had set up a bunch of rocks for cover at the mine entrance.

A shot rang out from the cave, and I heard one of the attackers scream in pain.

A loud cackle exploded from the mine. "That's all fer you, you rotten, skunk-livered pisspot!" Then Ned cackled again.

"How's your shooting, Fred?" Jake asked.

"I been known to bag me a deer for eatin'," he replied. "I ain't never shot no white man, though."

"Well, you're going to shoot a few today, Fred. Nate, you see that man, the one closest to the mine? He's a clear shot for you."

I never shot a man before, and I didn't want to start now. But it was my choice to be here, and he was trying to kill Ned and Whitetail.

Jake put his hands on my shoulders. "I know it isn't right," he said to me. "But it has to be done. You wanted to protect what's yours."

"I know," I said miserably.

"I want you to lie flat on this rock. Line up the back sight with the front sight. When I tell you to shoot, squeeze the trigger. Don't yank on it. It should surprise you when it goes off. Everyone's counting on you, Nate."

I got myself all set up on the rock and set up the sight in the middle of the man's back.

"Jake?" I said, not daring to move. "I'll be shooting a man in the back."

"Yes," he said. "You will. You're not in a saloon, Nate. This is a battle situation. A battle is never clean nor pretty. And it's never fair, not if you want to win."

"But he won't have a chance!"

"No, he won't. Nor would he give you one. Nate, these men are trying to kill someone they don't even know, just for a few dollars. Now, we're going to make what's called an uncoordinated attack. That means Ned doesn't know we're coming, so he can't cover us. So we're depending on you."

Jake and Fred slowly made their way down the canyon, while I stared at the sights until they blurred. Shaking it off, I saw Jake and Fred get into position behind the claim-jumpers.

It was over in a few seconds. The claim-jumpers never had a prayer. Jake and Fred shot the first two at the same time and before the rest of them could turn around the second two were down.

"Shoot!" Jake yelled.

The feller who was my target had turned around to see who was shooting from behind, and I had a quick sense of relief that I wouldn't be getting him in the back, after all.

"Shoot!" Jake yelled again.

My feller had taken aim at Jake, so I did what he told me; I pulled back real slow and easy on the trigger and felt the stock punch me in the shoulder. My feller just seemed to flop down out of sight.

"Come on down, Nate!" I heard Jake shout.

"Well, I'll be goddamned 'n drawn 'n quartered 'n kicked right smack in the willies!" Ned shouted as he ran out of the mine. "Say, Marshal, that were one hell of a encirclement, right out of the book!"

"You mounted your defenses just right," Jake said.

"These skunk-asses all gone to Jesus?"

They had. I'd seen men shot and even killed before— saloons can get rough, especially during the rains when everyone is bored and cranky—but never this many at the same time. I avoided looking at the man I shot, but everyone else seemed pretty dead, all right.

Jake put his arm around me. "You did just fine, Nate. You probably saved my life. Now put it away."

"They're a pretty ragged-looking bunch," I said, and they were. They all looked skinny and hungry and hard. "They just . . . none of 'em look like they'd eaten a good meal in days!"

"Probably not," Jake said. "But what kinda men murder someone just for the price of a meal?"

"Piss on 'em, kid," Ned said. "I killed better men 'n these. Lotsa Yankees, 'n they meant less harm 'n these bushwhackers. If I go to hell, it ain't gonna be over these horse pies."

"This one still alive," Fred called.

It was the man I shot. I didn't want to look, but I couldn't stop myself. He had one of those hard, lived-in faces, the kind that hadn't seen a good day in a long time. It was a scary, desperate face, the kind capable of just about anything. It was a face that would have made me afraid.

"Water," the man croaked.

Jake went over and knelt beside him. His chest was all bloody. All because of me.

"Who hired you?" Jake asked.

"Water . . . please."

"It'll kill you."

"But I won't die thirsty."

"Can't argue that," Ned said. "Give 'im some goddamn water."

Jake took out his canteen and poured some water on the man's cracked lips.

"Who hired you? Was it Wilson?"

"Which one a you done shot me?"

"Who hired you?"

"Yeah . . . was 'at Wilson sumbitch. He give us twenny-fi' dollar a piece."

"Twenty-five dollars!" Ned shouted. "That cheapskate sumbitch. He thinks my hide ain't worth but twenty-five dollars?"

The dying man's eyes sought me out. *"You* killed me. Why, you're jus' a boy!"

I almost said I was sorry, but it struck me as foolish. So I didn't say anything.

"Forget it, kid," he said weakly. "You done me a favor."

"Hell of a favor," Ned commented.

"Somebody pray for me!" he shouted louder than it seemed he could.

"Goddamn, you're taking longer to die 'n Julius Caesar," Ned said.

"I been a murderer an' thief an' I'm goin' t' hell!"

"Well, you mustn't keep the devil waitin', son."

I was finding this a little hard to take. I noticed the rifle in my hands and threw it down.

"I'll pray for you, mister," I said, but it was too late. He made a funny noise in his throat, and then his eyes seemed not to see anymore. Jake closed his eyes for him and got up. "These things happen, Nate. Put it behind you."

I nodded miserably. I wondered if I ever again would enjoy the kind of good night's sleep I'd been having lately. It seemed to me I'd never again close my eyes without seeing that man begging me to pray for him.

"Forget him, kid," Ned said in what I guessed was a kindly tone. "He's playing poker with Ol' Scratch as we speak. Now for them damn Wilsons!"

6

I HAD THOUGHT that Jake would ride straight from the mine right to the Wilsons' ranch and clap old Alvin Wilson in irons, but he didn't. Instead, he had Ned and his helpers remain at the mine as if nothing had happened. Old Ned went blue in the face when Jake told him he wasn't going to arrest Wilson, nor were they even going over there for a shoot-out, which was what old Ned wanted most of all.

"Why in the hey-ull not?" Ned demanded.

"We are not in the murder business, Ned," Jake replied evenly. "If I go over there to arrest him, I am not within my legal rights. We do not have enough evidence against him for an arrest."

"What 'n a goddamn hell do ev-i-dence hafta do w' it?"

"It has to do with the *law,* Mr. Harper."

"Who ever heard of a marshal goin' by the law?" Ned wondered.

"You just worry about your mine," Jake said. "I'll handle Wilson."

But he didn't handle him right away. The first thing Jake did when he got back to town was shut himself in his office to write a report. Myself, I went back to the shop, where Mr. Levy had a stern look for me, which I deserved, having run off without telling him. But I must've looked pretty miserable, because he softened almost immediately, like he could tell something really awful had just happened to me. He just asked me if I'd et, and when I said I weren't hungry, he quietly put me back to work.

A few days passed, and it didn't seem like Jake was going to do *anything* about the Wilsons. That all changed when we was having breakfast one morning at the hotel, and I seen Judge Hackett come in.

"Mornin', Judge," I said.

"That's Judge Hackett?" Jake whispered to me.

I nodded, and Jake stood up and said, "Good morning, Your Honor. Won't you join us?"

"You must be our new marshal," the judge said. "Greetings and salutations, Mr. Murchison."

That was the judge all over. No one knew who he really was or where he come from. He lived in a small house on the edge of town with a Negro girl was supposed to be his servant but everybody winked and stuck their tongue in their cheek over that one. When he weren't sloppy drunk, you could see him in his yard, reciting poetry whilst feeding his chickens. He always talked like he was saying poetry, even when he weren't.

The judge pulled out a seat and sat down, and Jake nodded for the waiter.

"Just coffee, my noble sentinel; I've had an ample repast in my own humble abode. Well, young Nathaniel, our own municipal Oliver Twist. Or is it Pip Pirrup?"

"How've you been, Judge?" I said.

"Ah, my boy, as well as can be expected when one resides in a cultural wasteland. I strongly suspect that other than Irma, my Nubian hausfrau—who, it should be said, is the target of much unfounded and unseemly speculation, unfounded not from any want of feeling on my part, but rather a sense of highly refined taste on hers—other than she, whose tender ministrations keep me relatively upright, the only keen minds in this town are seated at this table.

"To answer your question, young Nathaniel, I'm . . . comfortable, which is the best one can hope for with my age and my habits."

"Ain't seen you round town much these days," I said.

"Ah, for that, Irma may indeed take the responsibility. Hoping to cure, or at least, diminish my dipsomania, she has demanded that I write a book. The more time at quill and pen, she believes, the less opportunity and vigor will remain for my favorite pastime."

"What are you writing?" Jake asked.

"Ah," he replied with a sad smile. "A book on a subject in much demand in this territory. I'm anticipating brisk sales, particularly among the miners. The work in progress is an analysis of the development of the Restoration comedy on the London stage in the latter part of the seventeenth and early eighteenth centuries. Ah. Blank faces. I take it, then, that you have little interest in the Restoration comedy as a theatrical form?"

Well, I could only speak for myself, but the only thing I'd ever seen on a stage was a feller drinkin' kerosene and puttin' a fiery stick in his mouth. He must of been right thirsty by the time he was done.

But Jake said, "For a short-lived, transitional form, it had a great deal of impact on the English theater. Who do you prefer, Wycherly or Congreve?"

My eyes almost bugged out of my head, though not as much as the judge's. He looked happier than I'd ever seen him.

"Wonderful! Wycherly's *The Country Wife* is the period's definitive piece, but my favorite is Farquhar's *The Recruiting Officer.*"

"I know I'll enjoy your book when it's done, Judge."

"Now that I know someone might actually read it, I shall redouble my efforts."

"I hope to read it soon, Judge." Jake reached down into the leather valise he had brought with him and came out with a sheaf of papers. "I need your signature on these, Your Honor."

"Oh, my heavens! Legal work! A town marshal intimate with the workings of the law? You, sir, are an anomaly of the first water!"

"Simple police work, Judge. I'll need your signature on that, that, and that."

The judge took a pair of spectacles from his waistcoat. "All to the good, Marshal, but I thought I might peruse these documents first before investing them with the full authority and weight of the law."

"At your convenience, Judge."

The judge skimmed through the document as if it were routine and boring, like something he'd read a million times before. But when he got to the end, his shiny red face got even redder.

"Marshal," he said in a voice I'd never heard him use

before, "are you aware that if I sign these papers, I'm a dead man?"

"Not in this town, Judge. Not while I'm marshal. You'll have the full protection of the law. I'm sure that the governing body of this territory, which has ambitions of someday becoming a state, would not take the assassination of a public official lightly."

The judge got a sort of dreamy look in his eyes. "Assassination!" he said like it was a magic word. "You know, any poor fool can get himself murdered. Only great men are assassinated. I suppose every little boy *dreams* of being assassinated someday. Assassinated! Doesn't that, more than money or position, truly say you've arrived? But, no! I cannot be seduced!"

I don't know why he used that word on Jake. Jake sure didn't strike me as that way, though I wasn't so sure about the judge.

"Look, Judge," Jake said, "I can get on my horse right now and ride up to the capital. I'm sure the territorial magistrate in Prescott doesn't give a hoot in hell for the Wilsons and will be glad to sign this. But it's *your* job, Judge. You are referred to as *Your Honor*. Doesn't that mean anything to you?"

"Oh, you are cruel," the judge accused him. He leaned in close toward Jake. "Despite our brief acquaintance, I can see that you are a man of far more than average intelligence. You must be aware that I derive an income from Wilson's mine?"

"You'll still get your income, Judge. It's illegal for him to withhold it just because he's mad at you."

"Marshal. You are in *Arizona*. The law here is the law of the strong . . . and the armed."

Jake glared at him coldly. "Then quit," he said in that

low, icy voice of his. "Crawl inside your whiskey bottle and never come out again. I don't care if you want to allow yourself to become a bad joke. *But not the law.* You either enforce the law, or I'll remove you from office and replace you with someone who can."

"Can you do that?" I piped up, even though I should've kept my mouth shut.

"Yes, he can," the judge answered, not taking his fearful eyes off of Jake. "He can declare martial law in the event of civil disobedience and remove public officials if need be, as long as he informs the capital."

"What'll it be, Judge?" Jake leaned back like a man at a poker table calling with a royal flush. "One other thing, Judge," he said, when the judge didn't answer. "I'm from the East, but I guess you figured that out. And I'm educated, which means I come from a good family. As such, I have a few . . . connections. The connection I'm thinking of in particular sits on the board of regents at one of our nation's better universities. Universities teach literature. They tend to buy, and sometimes even publish, academic works . . . works such as, well, a book about Restoration comedies, for example. I'd be glad to put a word in the right ear. That is, if the book in question has merit and isn't just the mad ravings of a drunken has-been."

The judge took off his specs and tossed them on the table and rubbed his eyes. "The law is the law," he sighed. "And while it may be, at times, in Mr. Dickens's words, 'a ass,' it is still the basis of the fragile veneer we laughingly refer to as civilization."

He took out a fountain pen. "Very well, Marshal." He took a deep breath and signed his name in a big, round hand. "I wonder how many men in history have ever literally signed their own death warrant?"

"Thank you, Your Honor," Jake said. "You've done the right thing."

"I shall rest far easier in my grave with that benediction," the judge said. "No, don't go just yet. If I'm to be sent shortly to my eternal rest, let me go with memory of an intelligent conversation. Tell me, Marshal, why do you refer to the Restoration comedy as merely a transitional form? It sounds like the beginning of my next chapter. . . ."

I thought Jake would ride out to the Wilsons' ranch right away, but he didn't. Instead, he ambled over to the saloon and took Tom Tryer aside.

"I know you want to help your local lawman, *Tom,*" he said. "Don't you?" he gave Tom a little nudge. "I said, don't you?"

"Yes, sir, Marshal, I do," Tom said, which sounded to me like he didn't.

"Good!" Jake said, slapping him on the back a little harder than friendly-like. "Then you go tell your friend Alvin Wilson I want to see him in my office at his earliest convenience. Okay?" Jake smacked him again.

"I said, okay, damn it!"

"Why, thank you. I do appreciate a civic-minded fellow."

For the rest of the morning, Jake sat in a chair outside his office, smoking a cigar and exchanging greetings with everyone who passed by. Seemed like most of the good people in town liked having him around. Most of the bad element had either seen him in action or heard about him, so they were behaving themselves. The good folks appreciated this, and they said so.

Finally, 'long about midafternoon, the Wilsons come

riding into town. They was all there, all five boys and old Alvin Wilson hisself. Wilson was the kind of feller that if you was a foreigner living in Europe or someplace, you'd be scared to death if he was king. He was getting older, and he'd been living the good life for awhile now, so he wasn't so big and strong as he used to be. But he was plenty smart and plenty mean, though not the kind of mean that he yelled at people. He was the sort of mean guy who smiled a lot and acted friendly, but right behind that, you knew he meant business. You could see him as a king of Europe, telling somebody he was their friend and then leaving the room and whispering to his guards to chop the feller's head off.

I was outside the store setting up some new stock when they come riding in. They all hitched their horses up, and Jake stood. He and Alvin Wilson smiled and shook each other's hand like two fellers who deep-down hated each other's guts.

"Boys," Jake said. "Your father and I have to discuss a little business. Why don't you go on across the street and have a cup of coffee or something?"

Tad looked over at his dad, who nodded for them to go. Then Jake said, "Shall we step inside my office?"

"I'd be delighted," Wilson said like it were a really great idea.

I heard everything that went on next because I stood right next to the door and peeked around the window. Jake and Wilson both sat down, and Jake offered him a cigar, which Wilson turned down, and Jake didn't have one for himself. He took out the papers that the judge had signed for him.

"I'm sure you're a busy man, Mr. Wilson," Jake began, "so I'll make this as brief as possible. This document is a legal writ, a restraining order preventing you, your sons, or any agents in your employ from stepping within one hundred yards of the outer property boundary of the Harper mine."

Wilson turned red in less than a second. He had Tad's crazy eyes, or Tad had his, and they looked really crazy. "You can't do that!" he shouted.

"Oh, I certainly can, and I have," Jake said with a little smile.

Wilson calmed himself down and even managed to smile a bit himself. "I'll bring that to Prescott and appeal it in the territorial court, Marshal."

"Oh," Jake nodded like he agreed with him, "I would hope that you do. It's your legal right to do so."

"You have no evidence against me. I don't even know what this is about," Wilson said with a shrug, as if Jake picked on the wrong fellow but he was willing to be a good sport about it.

"Well," Jake said, agreeable, "it's about attempted murder, and the lesser but still serious charge of attempting to steal a claim. But you've also got a conspiracy charge, because you planned the attack on the mine for your own ends. These are very serious charges. Oh. One other thing. The men who were killed? You contributed to their deaths by sending them there in the first place. It's all very convoluted, Mr. Wilson, but you get my point."

"I still don't know what you're talking about," Wilson said, although he wasn't smiling as much. "What's any of this got to do with me?"

"Oh, I thought I'd mentioned that." He held up another sheet of paper. "This document is what is called a dying declaration. The courts feel that when a man is about to meet his maker, he tends to come clean about things, so they're inclined to believe what he says. This is the dying declaration of a Mr. John Doe, who stated shortly before he expired that you had paid him and seven others the sum of twenty-five dollars to kill Mr. Edward I. Harper and two Pima Indians in his employ. Of course, our territorial law is a bit fuzzy on dying declarations. I can't bring you to trial, because this declaration, as evidence, isn't enough to convict you, not on the murder charges.

"However, the law is kind. It will believe the dying declaration in the sense that you are implicated, and it does feel that Mr. Harper does in fact deserve the law's protection from you. So, with all that gotten out of the way, here is the restraining order, and I serve you with it now.

Wilson let the documents drop from his hands. "I ain't accepting it," he said.

"Well, that really doesn't matter, Mr. Wilson. You have actually touched it, and I've explained it to you. You might as well take it."

Wilson snatched it from the floor. "Who signed this? Hackett? Why I'll—"

"Assassination of a public official is a hanging offense, Mr. Wilson. Even in Arizona. Oh, and one other thing. I went to the city clerk's office and took a look at the incorporation papers of your mine. If Judge Hackett's ten percent royalties are not paid him when due, you will be charged with embezzlement of his share. I hope you'll keep that in mind."

Wilson stood up. "If there's nothing else, Marshal . . ."

"Just that Judge Hackett's and Mr. Harper's continued good health are very much your responsibility, Mr. Wilson. I know you won't take such a responsibility lightly."

Mr. Wilson smiled like he'd lost this one, but tomorrow was another day.

"And what of *your* continued good health, Marshal?"

"I'll pretend I didn't hear that, Mr. Wilson. And keep those children of yours in line. Their antics are beginning to bore me."

"As yours are beginning to bore me, Marshal. I'll see you again, sir. This matter is not concluded."

7

LOOKING BACK ON it now, 1881 was a eventful year, not just for me, but for Arizona, especially our part of it. At the very time all this was goin' on, we all got a chance to breathe easier because the eastern end of Pima County, which was the southeast corner of the territory where it bordered New Mexico, was cut off to form a new county. The new county, Cochise, had its seat at Bisbee, but the big-news place at the time was a town called Tombstone.

We was all pretty relieved that Tombstone was now some other county's problem. This was the year that matters came to a head between the Earps and the Clantons and everybody else. Tombstone was a boomtown like ours, but it was Paris, France, compared to our little place.

The reason why I bring up Tombstone, even though it ain't really a part of what happened to me here in Granger, is that everyone was watching what was going on there right close. Even the new president, Jim Garfield, and a little later, Chet Arthur kept an eye on things. Tombstone was going to hell fast, and the bodies were pilin' up like

there was still a war going on. It made us all feel funny,
like we was all a bunch of law-breakers. The president
threatened a couple times to bring in martial law, and
goodness knows he had the soldiers to do it. I read once
that one out of every five soldiers in the whole army was
stationed in Arizona to fight the Apaches. I'd a hated for
soldiers to come into Granger. They was worse'n cowboys, always drunk and fightin' and shootin' up the place,
and you couldn't complain to their officers, because they
wasn't much better. At least cowboys and miners do
something worthwhile when they ain't drunk. If we'd a
had soldiers in Pima County, they'd a been useless. The
Injuns down here was Pimas like Fred and Whitetail, and
they never hurt nobody. I always thought that Pimas was
pretty nice fellers. They just wanted everybody to leave
'em alone so they could go about their business.

Anyhow, in a silver boomtown like Tombstone, and
even one like ours—though not as much—there's a hell
of a lot of money a even slightly crooked lawman can
pull out for himself. The Earps wanted that money, just
like Old Man Wilson wanted his. And they was tough
enough to fight anyone who stood in their way for it.

Jake was different, though. In all the time I knew him,
I never saw any sign that he gave a damn about money.
It just didn't seem to interest him, was all. It was like I've
always been with liquor; I got nothing agin it, I just don't
partake of it myself. I like other things. Maybe, having
growed up in a saloon, I saw too many times men makin'
fools of themselves and even getting themselves killed
because of it. Well, that seemed to be Jake with money.
When he first become marshal, every Friday he'd get
these little envelopes from Miss Flora and Tom Tryer and
the other saloonkeepers and brothel-owners in town. And

every Friday, he'd make his rounds and give 'em right back. Soon everybody got the message, and the envelopes stopped coming.

It was lucky for him, too, because old Alvin Wilson started in on him right away. I remember the first thing he did, too, because I was right there when he did it. It weren't violent, but legal, just the way Jake would of done it.

Mr. Levy and I was going over the accounts when Mr. Wilson walked into the store. That was odd in itself because Mr. Wilson never did his own shopping; he had servants for that very purpose.

"Morning, Aaron," he said.

"Morning, Alvin," Mr. Levy said right back. "Anything I can get you today?" The two was so stiff with each other that you could tell they was enemies. I heard later that Mr. Levy once caught Virge Wilson stealing and threw him out of the store. Then Tad come in and tried to make something of it, but Mr. Levy lifted him up by his belt and collar and *really* threw him out. Then Earl come and tried to fight, but Mr. Levy took a club and knocked his wind out. Mr. Wilson then told his boys to leave Mr. Levy alone. Mr. Wilson and Mr. Levy had no use for each other, but neither was scared of the other.

"I come to see you in your official capacity," Wilson said.

"All right," Mr. Levy said.

"I'm a-callin' for a special election," Mr. Wilson said.

"A special election for what?" Mr. Levy asked.

"For town marshal."

"We have a town marshal," Mr. Levy said. "And he's doing a good job."

"I been up to Prescott," Wilson said. "I done some

looking into things. As mayor, you have the right to appoint a marshal on a in-terim basis only. A special election can be called at any time. Lookit Tombstone. They just done it."

Wyatt Earp's brother, Virgil, had been appointed marshal of Tombstone earlier that year. But he had just been soundly whupped in a special election like the way Mr. Wilson wanted. Then Wyatt run for Cochise County sheriff, and he got whupped, too, by a feller name of Johnny Behan. So Wyatt done stole Behan's girlfriend, Josephine Marcus. Tombstone was a complicated place.

"If'n you want, Aaron, I can get up a petition. How about you save me the trouble?"

Well, getting up a petition wouldn't be no trouble for Mr. Wilson. All he had to do was tell every one of his miners who wanted to keep his job to sign the thing.

Mr. Levy sighed. They wasn't nothing he could do to stop it. Mr. Wilson had the law on his side this time.

"Who do you plan to run against Jake?" he asked.

"Me?" Wilson said, like he didn't know what Mr. Levy was talking about. "I ain't gonna run nobody. I'm just a concerned citizen." After a long pause, he said, "My son Tad has always aspired to be a lawman. I think he'd be good at it."

My hair bristled at the thought of Tad Wilson as town marshal. Talk about foxes in a henhouse!

I ran next door to tell Jake what was what. Funny thing was, he didn't seem too concerned.

"It's the American process, young Nathaniel," he said. "Town marshal is an elective office. I was wondering when old Wilson would get around to it. It's the smart thing to do."

"But, Jake! *Tad Wilson* as marshal?"

"I never planned on staying here forever, Nathaniel," Jake said. "Not to belittle your hometown, but this place is something of a hole. If it weren't for men like you and Aaron Levy, Granger would be a lost cause along the lines of Gomorrah."

"Jake! You sound like you already done lost the election!"

Jake smiled and took out his pocket watch. "Stage is almost due. Come on, Nathaniel, let's take a little walk."

Jake always met the stage when it come into town. That way, he got to know who was new in town, just passing through, or who might be trouble. Well, it turned out that who got off the stage would be trouble, but not the kind of trouble Jake was expecting.

The stage had already put in at the Wells Fargo office, but there were only a couple people on it. Since the Benson stage had been robbed and one poor fella killed and more'n $2,000 in silver had been stolen, traveling by stage wasn't real popular these days.

Anyhow, they was a salesman-type feller with a heavy sample case and a older, whiskered codger. They both went straight to the hotel.

But they was also this young woman in a white muslin dress with a bustle and carrying a parasol. When she turned around, I saw she had these blond locks and a face pretty enough to make you go cross-eyed.

And I'll be go-to-hell if she didn't take one look at me and give me the biggest, widest, prettiest smile that ever made the ground under my feet turn into porridge.

"Why, you must be the industrious young Nathaniel," she cried in a sweet Southern accent. "And the famous Marshal Murchison! How kind of you to take the trouble to meet me! Why, you're just the way my daddy described you!"

That was the first time I ever saw Jake just a bit uncomfortable-like. "Ma'am? Your . . . father?"

"Oh, how rude of me not to introduce myself. I'm Lida Mae Williams. Well, that was my married name. Most tragic," she added with a little sigh, the kind that was more relieved than mournful. "My maiden name is Harper."

Jake and I both goggled. "You're . . . *Ned Harper's* daughter?" I exclaimed in a voice too high for someone my age. If I had to imagine Ned having a daughter, my mind sure wouldn't a come up with someone who looked like her.

"Why . . . yes! I've not seen my dearest papa in more than ten years! How is the darling lamb?"

Ned Harper . . . a darling lamb. Well, I guess anything is possible on this here earth.

"Your father is out looking after his . . . business interests," Jake said. "May I help you get settled first? Then it'd be my pleasure to drive you out to see him."

"Oh, you are a sweet man, Marshal. Are you married?"

Jake's eyes clouded. "No, ma'am."

"I see. You, too, have met with tragedy."

Well, that was the first I'd heard about Jake's ever having been married, but I'd always suspected it somehow.

"Come," Jake said. "We'll get you settled in at the hotel."

"If it's all the same to you, Marshal, I just need to change out of these gentle habiliments and into something more appropriate for rugged conditions. I'd like to visit that emporium across the street."

"That's where I work, ma'am," I said. "I'll be glad to fix you up with whatever you may need. And since you're Ned's daughter, credit shouldn't be a problem if you need it."

"Oh, credit," she dismissed it with a wave of her hand. "Although . . . hmmmm. We'll see. You may take my arm, Nathaniel."

Well, sir, I felt bigger'n all creation walking across the street with Lida Mae Harper on my arm. Of course, I felt a little bit smaller . . . and bigger at the same time . . . when I noticed that Rebecca Levy saw me and then pretended not to.

"Mr. Levy," I said when we got to the store, "this here's Lida Mae Harper. Ned's daughter."

"*Ned's* daughter?" he exclaimed.

"Why is everyone so surprised?" Lida Mae asked. "Everyone says I take after him."

We all found the ceiling pretty interesting after she said *that*. "This is the kindly Mr. Levy?" she asked. "My, my, this town is just chock-a-block filled with strong, handsome men!"

Just then, Rebecca had come into the store. She pretended like she was looking for something, but I could tell it was really to get a better look at Lida Mae.

"Is this your little girl, Mr. Levy? Why she's a vision!" Lida Mae took a look at me and then at Rebecca. "You'd best grab this young man up, child," she whispered to Rebecca, "or soon you'll be fightin' off the other girls with a stick."

"I'm very good with a stick," Rebecca replied. She took a pound of sugar and went out.

"I'd say that girl's sweet on you, Nathaniel," Lida Mae whispered.

I cleared my throat. "What do you need, ma'am?"

"Well, now, let's see. I know it's most unladylike, but I will require a pair or two of Mr. Levi Strauss's trousers. I'll also take one of them linsey-woolsey blouses, a pair a those boots—I do hope you have a size small enough— oh, and Mr. Levy, sir?" She picked up a leather hat and tried it on. "I do hope it is not against your sense of propriety, but I will require a firearm, preferably one of Mr. Colt's Yankee Army models in .45 caliber? I would be especially grateful if the grips were a checkered wood instead of pearl or ivory."

"I can change them out for you, if you'd like," Mr. Levy offered.

"You are most kind, sir. One other thing, Mr. Levy. Have you a two-shot derringer or perhaps a Merwin-Hulbert double-action revolver in .32 caliber? A lady cannot be too careful in these most difficult times."

"I'd say you like to be prepared for all contingencies," Jake said, speaking up for the first time.

"Being unprepared," she said, with a very slight edge to her voice, "can be most disagreeable. Especially in such wild country as this."

As Lida Mae went into the back room to change, I couldn't help but notice a strange look on Jake's face. I went over to him asked, "What's wrong, Jake?"

"I wonder what she really wants," he said, more to himself.

"How do you mean?" I asked him.

"I don't trust her," he said. Then he added with a kind of a weak smile, "I also don't trust myself."

"Why, Jake! You're sweet on her!"

He took me aside. "Nate, you're a smart kid. So I'll level with you. I think she's very attractive. Now, I can

assure you that I'm not the only fellow who ever thought
so. She, quite obviously, is aware of this, and she uses it.
I've no trouble with that—as long as she doesn't try to
use *me.*"

"What do you think she wants?"

"I don't know—yet. But remember, everybody wants
something. That could be good or bad, but she didn't
come out here just to renew her relationship with her father. Or else, why would she wait ten years? I'd also like
to know what happened to her husband."

"I shot him, is what happened," came a voice from the
back of the store. Lida Mae came out from the changing
area, looking even prettier despite the rugged clothes she
now wore. Mr. Strauss's trousers were tight on her, ac-
centuating the curve of her hips, and the effect was, well,
a bit bothersome—enough to make me wonder what kind
of husband I'd someday be to Rebecca if I could think
such thoughts about other women like I was thinking now.
Even a grown-up like Lida Mae Harper.

"Mr. Levy, sir, what do I owe you for these accoutre-
ments? With this be sufficient?" She took out a twenty-
dollar gold piece and held it up.

"Far more than sufficient," Mr. Levy said. "I'll get your
change."

"Please, sir, leave it on account. Or has my father any
outstanding debts at this establishment?"

He had, but I'd paid them myself with the first bag of
silver nuggets pulled from the mine.

"No, ma'am, his slate is clear, and his credit is good."

"Thank you, sir. My father has often mentioned your
many kindnesses, and here I find them all to be more than
true. Now, sir, may I borrow your young assistant? I'd
like to take him for a meal and talk about my father, with

whom he seems to have a special friendship."

That was news to Mr. Levy, who raised his eyebrows but nodded his permission. Mr. Levy was also known as a man who minded his own business.

"Marshal? Are you coming, sir?"

"Of course."

Some of Mr. Wilson's flunkies were already raising a banner over the street that said Elect Tad Wilson Marshal. It handed Jake a small laugh, but I didn't think it was all that funny. Wilson could buy Tad the election with little trouble, and Jake didn't even seem to notice. I wondered, all of sudden, what it was that *he* wanted.

Lida Mae surely attracted as much attention in the hotel dining room as she would have if she were naked, wearing trousers and a six-gun and a leather hat like she was. But Jake pulled out her chair for her, and when the food come, she ate daintily like the lady she was.

"I hate to bring up a delicate matter," Jake said. "But you were going to give me the particulars of the tragic event that occurred with your husband."

Lida Mae shrugged. "The only tragic thing about it is that I had to leave Virginia. I'm a wanted woman there, you see."

"Wanted?"

"For murder, sir. You—" She paused a moment. "You have no legal authority over me in that matter, do you?"

"None whatsoever. Although, if you're extradited, I can detain you for the U.S. marshal. But that seems highly unlikely."

"Very well. My husband was a drunk. A wealthy man, capable of great kindness and quite loving in his way. But liquor changed him. He would become . . . ineffective . . . in some ways, and he would express his deep frustration through violence—violence directed against my person."

"He beat you," Jake nodded.

"I still have scars, Marshal. I knew it was a sickness, I knew that he wasn't himself, but his bouts with sobriety became less and less frequent, and he stayed drunk most of the time.

"I was pregnant. I wanted a child more than anything. Well, sir, not to put too fine a point on it, he beat that baby from me. I can never have children again. I decided then and there that I would never tolerate another act of violence from him, and the next time it happened, I shot him. He died. I was arrested. I escaped. Therefore, sir, what I *want,* as I heard you wonder aloud back in Mr. Levy's emporium, is a new life. I cannot offer a man children, but I can provide love, understanding, and companionship. In return, I demand respect and gentle treatment."

"You should expect no less," Jake said.

"Very well, sir. Since I have been forthcoming with you, I think you may now pay me the same compliment. You are a melancholy man, sir. You carry it with you like a peddler's heavy load . . . and it surrounds you. A blind man could see it."

I started to get out of my chair. "You know what," I said, "it seems to me that you two have lots to talk about, and I'm not really—"

"No, stay," she said, putting her hand over mine. "You have been privy to my secrets, now it is the marshal's turn. Consider yourself the trusted friend who holds both shares of a wager. Marshal?"

"My wife was pregnant as well," Jake said. "She died in a fire. I was a police president in New York. Five Corners—the cesspit of the city." Jake spoke quickly, as though he was in a hurry to get it out and be done with it. "After that, I tried to forget through sheer hard work. There was a gang of dusters—"

"Dusters?" Lida Mae asked.

"Fellows who got themselves hopped on cocaine or opium. It made them crazy. They went on a rampage one night, robbing people, beating them, a reign of terror— and I brought in a squad to round them up. Well, most of them had guns, and it became . . . well, somewhat bloody. I was wounded that night, but I killed two of them . . . one of whom, it turned out, was younger than Nathaniel here. A lot younger. I went back to the station, took off my badge, and here I am."

"Wearing another badge," Lida Mae murmured softly.

Jake straightened up in his chair. "But not for long. I am being opposed for election by moneyed elements, and I do not have the inclination nor the desire to mount a campaign. I was headed for California, anyway. An old army friend has timber interests in Sonoma County and has asked me to come in with him."

"Jake!" I said. "Timber, for God's sake! You can't leave!"

Jake shrugged and looked straight into Lida Mae's eyes. They didn't say much after that, but they didn't have to.

I got up slowly, carefully, like they was in a big soap bubble and if I moved too fast I'd burst it. That's how I left them.

When I got back to the store, Mr. Levy seemed a bit nervous, like there was something he wanted to say but didn't know just how to go about it. We had a flurry of business, and when they left, he cleared his throat and said, "Uh, Nathaniel? There's something I want to discuss with you, if you don't mind."

"I don't mind, sir."

"Well, son, a lot's been happening lately, to you and me both. Whatever you're doing after store hours is your own business, of course. But I have a proposal you might want to consider."

"A proposal, sir?"

"How would you like to own a piece of this store?"

"Why, Mr. Levy! That would be wonderful! But I'm only . . . not even sixteen. Ain't I a little young?"

"Nathaniel, by now everyone in town knows how smart you are, how much you've helped me here. You won't be almost sixteen forever."

"But, sir, why now?"

"Sit down, Nathaniel." We pulled up some chairs near the stove and cracker barrel. There was no fire in the stove because it was summer, but it was still the place we sat around.

"Nathaniel, this town is getting to be like a wild train run off its rails. Sooner or later, it's gonna crash into something. Now with Tad Wilson running for marshal and Jake not seeming to care . . ." he trailed off and didn't say anything else.

"But you're mayor, sir! You can do something—"

"Not if all the folks with money are against me and all the good people are afraid. Anyway, Nate, this town's whole economy depends on silver. What happens when it runs out?"

"You think it'll run out?"

"Of course it will. It always does. Well, son, I have a wife and daughter. I worry about them all the time. I want Rebecca to grow up someplace that isn't so . . . well, someplace a little more civilized. I've been looking into opportunities in San Francisco. But at the same time, it wouldn't be right to leave you high and dry."

My heart sank. "San Francisco? But, sir, that's six, seven hundred miles from here!" I couldn't imagine living in a town without Rebecca. What would happen? Who the hell could I possibly marry if not Rebecca?

"It's not anything nailed down just yet," he said. "But I want to make you a partner in this store, and then you can buy it from me outright when we leave."

"Mr. Levy," I said. "You don't have to do that. You worked hard to build up this business. You don't have to give me a partnership. I can buy into the place right now."

I shouldn't of told him that, but it was out, and I decided I might as well tell him everything. "I've got twelve hundred dollars in Mr. Stout's bank right now." That was how much I'd earned from the mine already. There was more, but I'd given it to Ned to put back in the mine.

"Why, Nate? Where would you get that kind of money?"

I sighed. "From Ned Harper's mine, sir. I own thirty-three per cent of it. That's where I been goin' in my time off."

"You . . ." He stopped talking and started laughing. He tried to stop, then he got up and walked around the store, falling over stuff until he got ahold of himself again.

"Oh, Nathaniel," he said. "You're gonna own this whole town someday. I just know it. I'm so proud of you, my boy."

"Sir I'm glad," I said a little nervously. "But there's something else. Something to do with why it'd be just awful if you left town."

"I see," he said. "What is it?"

"Sir, I know I come from . . . well, where I come from. But I think I've been a honest man despite that. Sir, please don't be insulted or angry, though if you want me to leave your employ, I'll understand. Mr. Levy, I've loved Rebecca ever since I can remember, and even though I'm too young to ask for her hand, I'd like your permission to court her. I will treat her like the fine lady that she is and see to it that she never goes hungry nor feels unhappy about anything ever, and I've already taken steps to provide for her. Sir, no one could ever love Rebecca like I do."

Mr. Levy's smile vanished. I thought for a second he was mad at me. He took out his pipe and went through a long howdy-do of filling it, tamping it down and then lighting it to his satisfaction. All of which got on my nerves. If he was gonna yell at me, I wished he'd do it already.

"You say," he puffed, "that you love Rebecca. Does she feel the same about you?"

"I don't know, sir. I think she . . . feels highly about me, but I wouldn't know otherwise. We never . . . been alone together or anything. She kissed my cheek once, but that was after I helped her with her reading, and she was real happy about it. I guess that don't count, though."

He nodded. "You know that we have plans for her," he said. "There aren't many boys around here of our faith. That's another reason why I want to move us to San Francisco."

"Sir, I was raised with no faith. I never been in a church or nothing. But I'd do whatever Rebecca wanted."

"A lot of folks don't hold with our faith, Nathaniel. It hasn't been so bad out here, because people are so busy just trying to get by that they can't waste time with such foolishness. But still, there always comes a time when someone'll try to make things rough on you. It happened to me in the army. Lucky I was big enough and mean enough to put a stop to it when it happened."

"You was mean?" I couldn't help smiling. Mr. Levy'd walk halfway across the desert to give a thirsty man water, but I couldn't imagine him cross with anyone. Still, he was a big fella, almost as big as Jake. And he did face down the Wilsons when the time come.

"Nathaniel, in Tennessee, General Grant ordered all Jewish peddlers out of the state. Not because they had done anything wrong—but because his brother had been bilked by a fellow who happened to be of that faith. So he took it out on everybody. That man became president of the United States. Now, I ask you, Nathaniel, think hard. Do you really want to buy a peck of trouble like that?"

"Sir, I'm in love with your daughter. Have I your permission to court her?"

"Nathaniel, you're not even sixteen. She may not be the only girl who'll ever strike your fancy."

"Sir, I grew up around pretty girls. Why is it that none of *them* ever struck my fancy? No, sir. Rebecca is the only girl for me, has been since the first time I ever saw her. And as for my age, Mr. Levy, I've had a very busy almost-sixteen years."

He chewed on that for awhile. "Nathaniel, you said before that you've already provided for her. May I ask how?"

"I don't actually own thirty-three percent of the mine. I own twenty-three. The other ten percent is in Rebecca's name, and I've already got her an account in the bank with almost five hundred dollars in it."

The pipe flew out of his mouth. "You what!"

"It's hers, sir. She's welcome to it. Of course, there's gonna be more."

"But, Nathaniel, you don't even know if she wants you!"

"Mr. Levy," I said slowly, "when I was about eight or nine, I remember sweeping off the front planks of the saloon, and the kids would come walking by from the schoolhouse. They'd rag me all the time, call me names like whore-boy and Mary-britches and laugh and even throw shit at me. All except Rebecca. She always said, 'Hi, Nate,' and smiled at me. Sometimes she'd even give me a apple or a piece a licorice from your store. And I remember once, even though the other kids were ragging on her for not ragging on me, she came over and patted my shoulder and said, 'I wish they'd let you come to school with us.' Well, sir, after I was done sweeping, I went into the barn and sat down and started crying, crying to beat the band, and when I stopped I said, 'I love you, Rebecca,' even though she weren't there. I never said that before nor since, but I meant it then, and I mean it now."

Mr. Levy didn't say nothing for quite awhile, and then we saw a customer looking around at the display out front. We both got up, but before we went out, he put an arm around my shoulder.

"Come over for dinner tomorrow night," he said. "If it's all right with Rebecca, you can sit on the porch and talk about whatever it is kids in love find to talk about."

8

IF I'D A had any doubts that Lida Mae came out of the same blood as old Ned, they were pretty much flattened by the first words they said to one another when we arrived at the mine.

"Why, Papa," she cried. "You look like something a dog left on the bottom porch step! What in the hell happened to you?"

"Lida Mae!" he shouted. "Heard you shot that lowdown sumbitch Williams! You pull the trigger twice to make sure he was dead?"

I noticed that she was holding her breath while she hugged her papa. "Daddy! Don't you ever bathe?"

"Hell, no, I don't never bathe! You see a bathtub out here? I get so's I can't stand it, I jump in that stream over there."

He pointed to a dry creek bed.

"It's dry, Papa."

"Well, that ain't my fault, is it? Arizona ain't got no water—that's big news."

"I can stand it if you can," Lida Mae said.

"That's my little girl," Ned said. "Come on, I'll show you the family business. This here Injun's Fred, and that there's Whitetail."

"What about the other miners?"

"What other miners?"

"You mean you're working this mine with just three men?"

"Well, four on Sundays. That's when old Nate here helps us out."

"Why, that is preposterous! Daddy, you need more men!"

That's what I had always thought, but where would we get 'em from?

"I think I have an—" She stopped suddenly, and in what had to be less than a second, I heard a gunshot.

"Would one of you fine gentlemen please dispose of . . . that?"

Lida Mae's Colt was smoking in her hand. A few feet away was a rattlesnake without no head.

"Where'd you learn to shoot like that?" Jake asked.

For an answer, Lida Mae dug into her purse and came out with a wrinkled and faded old photograph. The subject was a young, smooth-shaven Confederate Army officer.

I looked at the photo and then at Ned—a couple or three times. There was a resemblance, mostly around the eyes. "Ned? Was this you?"

"Still is, goddamn it." He snatched the picture from my hand and regarded it with a grunt. "Young 'n stupid," he murmured.

"And very handsome," Lida Mae said. "I remember the day you rode off to the war. I was only eight—"

"You was *ten.*"

"Thank *you,* papa. Anyhow, it was glorious! The only time I ever saw Grandpa with tears in his eyes."

Ned made a sour face. "I'll tell ya something about yer grandpa one a these days. An' as for glorious—"

"I know, Daddy. I'm just sayin' what it felt like to me at the time."

"What it *felt* like? Well, I hope it didn't feel like yer grandpa was standin' too close!"

"Let's change the subject, shall we, Papa?"

"Yore the one brought up the old bastard—"

"Your *father*—"

"Yeah, well, don't nobody hold it agin' me. I ain't got time fer this. You wanna work, or what?"

"I was thinkin', Papa—"

"God damn, you sound just like yer mother!"

"Well, I was. You need more men—"

"Thank you kindly. Now tell me somethin' I don't know—like where the hell I'm s'posed to get 'em? Every goddamn Welshman, Irishman, 'n Cornishman in southern Arizona who ain't in Tombstone is workin' for Wilson."

"So?"

Jake spoke up. "Miss Harper, are you suggesting that your father raid Wilson for miners?"

She put a hand over her breast. "Why, Jake, I thought this was supposed to be a free country! Can't a man work where he pleases?"

"How do you think old Wilson is going to react? You might be buying your father a great deal of trouble."

"How many men does Wilson have working for him right now?" Lida Mae asked.

" 'Bout two hunnerd," Ned figured.

"And how many do you need?"

"Aw, hell, I guess I could make do with twenty, thirty. Nate? How much a yore share you wanna reinvest?"

I was surprised and a little flattered to be included in grown-up conversation. But then, I had paid for it. "All of it, if it turns out to be worth it," I said. "Would you mind giving up a small share?"

"A slightly smaller share of a hell of a lot is better than a bigger share a not so much," Ned said.

"All right," I said. "I got me a idea. Jake, I gotta get back to town."

"You boys go on ahead," Lida Mae said. "I'll see you in a day or two. My papa's going to teach me the family business."

I never got over the fact that a grown man like Jake used to confide in a kid like me, but he always did. It made me a little bold. Sometimes I would ask him about things that were clearly none of my business. He never got mad, though. Usually, he just laughed.

"Are you and Miss Lida Mae sweet on each other?" I asked him as we rode away in the wagon.

He chuckled, just like I thought he would. "Well, I think it's safe to say that we both like what the other sees in a mirror," Jake replied. "Let me ask *you* a question. Why do you feel the way you do about Rebecca?"

A small rat spooked one of the horses, and I had to jerk on the reins to steady him. I grew up around horses, feeding and washing them and all that, but I was one happy feller when the auto-mobile got itself invented twenty years later. I was one of the first in Arizona to buy one, and my life has been wonderfully free of horse shit ever since.

"What was that?" I asked him as the horses steadied in my grip.

"Rebecca. What makes you feel the way you do about her?"

"I don't know," I said.

"She's pretty, isn't she?"

Yeah, she was, but so was Ashley Stout and plenty of other girls in town. Why her and not one a them? "Somethin' about her, I guess," I said finally. "I just always knew, if I ever saw Rebecca cry, my heart'd just fall right outta my chest. I guess it's 'cause . . . she's good. Yeah, I guess that's it."

"Well, you're way ahead of me," Jake said. "Lida Mae makes my blood rush like no woman since Elsie—my wife. But I always knew what Elsie was thinking. I'm not so sure about Lida Mae. And I can't court a woman I don't trust."

"You'd also feel a little odd if Ned was your father-in-law," I needled him.

He laughed outright at that one. "Yes, young Nathaniel," he said patting my shoulder, "I guess you do have me there."

I had a little bit of luck when I got back to town, because Emlyn Jones, the very fellow I was looking for, happened to be in the shop.

"Thank you for the denim trousers, Mr. Levy," Emlyn was saying in his Welsh accent. I could listen to him all day; it was like hearing a flute go up and down the scales. Emlyn Jones was one of the foremen at Wilson's mine and was probably the best working miner in Arizona. Wilson paid him beans, but the Welsh, who most people thought was Irish, couldn't be choosy about their jobs.

"Are you sure one pair will be enough, Emlyn?" Mr.

Levy asked. "You go through those pants faster than a weevil."

"Aye, but that's all I can afford for the present."

Mr. Levy shook his head and turned back to the trouser shelf. "Pay me when you can," Mr. Levy said, handing him another pair.

"Ah, now you've put me in an uneasy position with your generosity, Mr. Levy," Emlyn said. I stood there, enjoying the tones of Emlyn's voice trilling up and down. "You see, I have enough in the envelope for another pair of pants—but not for pants . . . and pints. I've much silver dust in my throat, sir. It must be washed away."

Mr. Levy finally gave in to laughter. "Emlyn—take both pair of pants and get out of here. And enjoy your beer."

"T'is a dreadful dearth of good men like you, Aaron Levy. My compliments to your beautiful family."

I stopped Emlyn outside the store. "Emlyn. Can I have a word?"

"From a blabbermouth like myself, Nathaniel, you may have threescore and ten."

"Could you come around the back? I'll meet you there." As far as I knew, the Wilsons didn't know I was in on Ned's mine, but I couldn't be sure. Anyhow, it wouldn't hurt to play it safe.

Emlyn looked surprised at my strange request but simply nodded. He met me around the back of the store and looked at me expectantly, not saying anything.

Well, I'd never stolen another man's worker before, and I didn't know quite how to go about it. So I just spoke my mind.

"It ain't none a my business, Emlyn, but how much does Wilson pay you?"

"Why do you ask, Nathaniel? Is usury another of your many talents?"

"Just want to know. You don't have to tell me if you don't want."

Emlyn sat on a barrel, took a deep breath, and looked up at the darkening sky. "T'is so lovely here! Back home, in the Rhondda Valley, there was beauty as well, a green beauty though it was, but it was so cold and so damp. We'd come out of the mine of an evening with coal dust in our lungs, and yet the dampness and chill would only make it worse. That's why we Welshmen like to sing, Nathaniel. Give our lungs some air, clean them out. My father and my uncles, all of them sang like nightingales. And still the black lung got them in the end. I've silver dust and God knows what else in mine, but the dry, sweet air of Arizona won't kill me as quickly.

"The cheap, slave-driving bastard Wilson pays me eight dollars a week. His going rate is six, but as a foreman, I'm entitled to another two. Why? Have you a better offer?"

"I—" I stopped. No use letting the cat all the way out of the bag. "Ned Harper does. He can't be here, so he asked me to talk to you. He wants you as his mining chief. He'll pay you—" I stopped and took a deep breath. "He'll pay you twenty dollars a week and give you three percent ownership in the mine."

He whistled softly. "Well," he said, " 'tis a pleasant thing to be wanted. I've heard of old Ned's good fortune. And how many men does he need?"

"How many can you bring with you?"

"That I can trust? Twenty. Perhaps twenty-five. The twenty-five best in the mine, of course. You'll pay them—"

"Twelve dollars a week," I said.

"Double. 'Tis a good beginning. And bonuses?"

"Bonuses?"

" 'Tis your doing, young Nathaniel. You've made me an owner, now I must think like a bastard. My lads work long and hard, coax a hell of a lot more silver out of that mine than you ever dreamed, they should be rewarded for it."

"Fair enough," I said. "We have a deal, then?"

He extended a huge, callused hand. "We've a deal."

"When can you and your men start?"

"Why, tomorrow, Nathaniel. I've worked for bastards long enough. Now I'm going to work for the biggest bastard of them all: myself."

"Old man Wilson'll be madder 'n a sick dog," I said, more to myself.

"Old man Wilson's a fool," Emlyn said. "He forgot the one most important rule of mining."

"Yeah? What's that?"

"Never cheat a Welshman, or you've made an enemy for life."

I plum forgot that I had been invited to the Levys' house for dinner, and I had just enough time to get myself back to the hotel to clean up before going over there. On the way, I cursed myself for forgetting to buy presents for them, but it was already too late.

I couldn't help but notice that I was treated just a little different by Mrs. Levy and Rebecca herself. Mrs. Levy was very polite, almost formal, and Rebecca had trouble looking straight at me. It felt a little odd, but it gave me a nice kind of shiver inside, like all of a sudden Rebecca was the kind of shy that you get when you're sweet on somebody.

Dinner was really formal, with Mrs. Levy and Rebecca damn near falling over themselves to refill my glass or get me more vegetables or meat. I never had anybody do that for me before, and I'd be lying if I said it didn't agree with me. We were all pretty quiet through most of the meal, and I guess Mrs. Levy finally had enough of that.

"Nathaniel, Rebecca has been doing wonderfully in school since you helped her with her reading problem. I don't know how to thank you."

"Mama!" Rebecca protested.

"It's true," Mr. Levy said. "She's at the top of her class right now."

Rebecca put down her knife and fork and rolled her eyes and sighed.

"I always figured you was the smartest girl in town anyhow, Rebecca," I said. "And the prettiest."

"Is that a fact?" she replied, sounding *exactly* like Lida Mae Harper. "My, my, Nathaniel, how you *do* talk!"

I started laughing and had to put a napkin to my mouth to avoid any embarrassing accidents.

"Mr. Levy," Rebecca continued in her Lida Mae voice, "do you suppose I could have that Bowie knife ovuh theah, and that Winchester rifle theah, that double-barreled shotgun up theah, oh, an' that cute ol' Gatling gun in the corner?"

By now we was all laughing so hard we couldn't eat. "Rebecca, stop that!" Mrs. Levy said, but there was a smile playing around her mouth.

"Marshal Murchison," Rebecca continued, "would you considuh bein mah next husband? I promise I'll only shoot you in the foot . . ."

"Come on, Rebecca," I said, grinning though I was, "that ain't fair. She's a nice lady, and she thinks very highly a you. She told me so."

"I think Rebecca's jealous," her father said.

"Well," I replied, before Rebecca could say anything, "she don't have nothing to be jealous about."

Nobody knew what to say to that, and it shut everybody up. We just started eating away again until we was done. Finally, Mr. Levy got up and said, "Nathaniel and I will retire for a bit, if you ladies don't mind."

For an answer, Mrs. Levy shooed us out of the room. We went into Mr. Levy's study where he lit the lamp and used the same match for a cigar. "Oh, I'm sorry, Nathaniel, would you like one? You are a man of means now, and if you'd like to smoke, feel free."

Well, I never had, and I wasn't ready to start just yet. "No, thank you, sir," I said.

"I don't like the idea of your going out to that mine without protection," he said. "There's lots of rattlesnakes . . . and other types of snakes. The kind that walk."

"Well, sir, I mostly go with Jake," I replied.

"Nevertheless," he said, "I'd like you to have this." He pointed to his desk, where a gleaming Colt six-gun was snug inside in a new cowhide leather holster that was coiled on top. The loops already had bullets in them.

"I got a shipment of army surplus," he said. "I worry about you out there, son."

"It's wonderful," I said with difficulty. I was going to try the thing on, but I thought of the man I killed up at the mine and couldn't touch it.

"Go ahead, put it on," Mr. Levy said.

"I thank you, sir. It's . . . it's the greatest present I ever had." Also the *only* present I ever had. "Can I keep it here or at the store? I'll put it on Sundays when I go out to the mine."

"Are you sure you don't want to put it on now?"

"Oh, no sir, I couldn't. But I surely thank you, I really do." I felt pretty awful, because I was sure that I was hurting Mr. Levy's feelings, but I couldn't have touched that gun at that moment if a rattlesnake come through the door.

"That's all right, Nathaniel," Mr. Levy said. "I'll keep it in the store under the counter, and it's yours whenever you want it. We'll speak no more about it. Now then, on to other business. I've been thinking about Jake's election."

"That's more'n he has," I replied.

"I don't believe he thinks he has a chance to win," Mr. Levy said. "He probably thinks Alvin Wilson will buy the election for Tad."

"It's possible," I said. "Look what happened to Virgil Earp over to Tombstone," I said.

"Tombstone's different," he said. "The Earps have a lot of enemies in town. It's a much bigger place, too. But everybody here likes Jake. There's no reason for him to lose, even if Wilson makes everyone in his mine vote for Tad."

"So you think he'll try to rig it somehow."

"I do," Mr. Levy said. "I think we need a disinterested third party to count the ballots, make sure they're counted right. He's got to be honest, and he's got to be tough enough not to be afraid of the Wilsons."

"I guess that's you," I said.

"Nice of you to say, Nathaniel. But I'm not disinterested. I'll pack up and leave five minutes after Tad Wilson is elected. No, I have another idea."

"Well, what is it, Mr. Levy?"

"Nathaniel, I think at this stage of the game, you ought to start calling me Aaron, don't you?"

It was a clear, sweet night, and there was no one on the street that Rebecca and I could see. It was funny, but we was holding hands, which we just started doing without a thought. But it didn't feel funny. It felt like I'd been holding her hand for years. It just felt right.

"Mr. Stout's working late," I remarked as we passed the bank.

"He always does," Rebecca said.

"Tom Tryer's seems to be pretty quiet," I said.

"Nate, are you giving me the grand tour? I live here, too, you know."

"Just makin' conversation," I said.

"Uh-huh. So, Nate," she said out of the blue, "you want to court me, do you?"

"I thought that's what I been doing."

"Oh, really? I'd've thought you might want to let *me* in on it."

"I thought you knowed. Okay," I said. "I'd like to court you. Is that all right?"

"And when did you decide this?" she asked.

I stopped and did some figuring. "Oh, I guess . . . when I was about eight or nine, so six, seven years ago."

"You've wanted to court me since you were nine years old?"

"No," I replied. "I've wanted to *marry* you since I was nine years old. The courtin' is just something to get out of the way first."

"Oh," she said in a very small voice. We walked a little

more, and then she stopped and said, "You want to *marry* me?"

"I have had that in mind, yes'm."

"What on earth for?"

"What for? I don't know. I figured we'd get married and live together and have kids and I'd work real hard and get rich and build us a real swell house and we'd live in it and laugh a lot. Oh, and I guess I'd get to kiss you once in a while."

"Do you want to kiss me?"

"Hell, yes."

"Why?"

"I figured I might like it enough to do it again. Are you asking me to?"

"Yes."

"In the middle of the street?"

"Who's going to see us?"

She put her lips up in a little pout, and I kissed her real quick. I liked the way her lips felt. That's the funny thing about kissing somebody—a girl, I mean. It never feels quite the way you'd expect, but it's always better'n you thought it would be.

Then, after I kissed her, we sort of looked in each other's eyes, and the world got real different and serious and growed-up. That's when I kissed her again, I mean we both kissed, and for a long time. And it would have lasted a lot longer if I didn't get this real funny feeling below the waist that I'd get after a good dream, and I broke it off.

"Well," she said, in a kind of out-of-breath voice. "Did you?"

"Did I what?"

"Did you like it?"

"Oh, yeah," I replied, a little out of breath myself. "I liked it just fine. I think this courting deal agrees with me. I guess we're engaged, then, huh?"

"You have to ask me first."

"Would you like to be engaged to me, Becky?"

"Yes, I would," she said.

"Well, that settles it then." I tried to be serious, since I was a real growed-up, engaged man with responsibilities now, but I felt this big stupid smile spreading all over my face.

"I'd best take you back," I said.

"All right," she said. "We're engaged! Goodness, that sounds very . . . different. I'll be Mrs. Nathaniel—Nate? I don't even know your last name!"

"Neither do I," I said. "I ain't got one . . . at least, not as far as I know."

"You must have a last name," she said. "We can't go around as Mr. and Mrs. Nate."

"But I'm a orphan," I said. That was the first time I had ever called myself that, and I didn't like it much.

"Well, maybe you have a birth certificate," she said. "That'd tell you who your folks were. Or your mom, anyway. You could take her name."

"What's a birth certificate?" I asked her. I'd never heard of such a thing.

"Why, Nate! Everybody has a birth certificate. That's how the county keeps track of everybody."

"You mean, I can find out who my folks were?" The idea plum knocked me over. "How do I go about it?"

"I'm not sure. But a good start would be to write to the county clerk's office in Tucson. That's if you were born here."

"I think I was. I been here ever since I can remember. So they'll tell me?"

"They'll tell you if they have your birth certificate."

"Well, wouldn't that be something!" I was still kind of at sixes and sevens. To tell the truth, I'd never even thought of myself as having parents. I just thought I got born and someone dumped me at Tom Tryer's. The thought of two people . . . aw, it was too much. "Maybe I'll write them tomorrow," I said.

"You do that," Rebecca said. "I'd sure like to know who it is I'm going to marry."

"You're marryin' *me*, Mrs. Nate."

9

EMLYN JONES AND his miners changed the look of the place almost overnight. This was because the Harper mine went from being just a three-man operation into a full-blown mining camp. Now there was almost thirty people living in tents near the mountain, and they had to eat. They wouldn't be getting into town any too often anymore, so there was a lot of things that had to be brought to 'em. I had to dig into my account at Mr. Stout's bank to get a lot of those things, but I figured I'd make that money back soon enough.

It occurred to me that a rancher, when he was moving cattle, took a chuck wagon along for the ride, so I figured it'd be easier on a feller not to be moving all the time. It worked out pretty good, although we had to build a small corral for the cattle.

On Sundays, I would take orders from the men for necessities from Mr. Levy's store, and sometimes I'd bring a keg of beer or a case of whiskey back with me, too. Once a fellow came by trying to start up a faro game, but

Ned run him off, saying at least let the fellas get back to town and have a good time before they were skinned for their wages.

The mine's overall take jumped over the moon once Emlyn and his men got settled in. The only thing still slowing us down was that our smelting method was still pretty rough and inefficient. They weren't much we could do about that, though. Ned kept banging it into my head that silver wasn't gold, and it was a hell of a lot tougher to coax it out of the rock.

Lida Mae turned out to be a bigger help than anyone thought she'd be. She wasn't afraid to go down into the mine and mix it up with the fellers, but we soon discovered that she was even better at running things, handling the money end, and driving hard bargains with the suppliers who discovered the camp and found a new market for their wares. You might of thought that she'd feel a little scared being surrounded by lonely men, but they was all gentlemanly with her. Maybe the fact that Ned said he'd shoot anyone a new butthole who acted less than polite with her had something to do with it. The miners was mostly Welsh and Irish, see, and where they come from, they didn't learn much about guns.

But I believe it was more the fact that Lida Mae simply knew how to act around men. It was a way she had about her; a feller would feel good talking to her because he had the attention of a pretty lady—but at the same time, he felt protective about her instead of dangerous. Also, the idea that Jake visited several times a week escaped no one's attention, and nobody wanted to make him mad . . . no one with sense, anyway.

In the meantime, I wrote away to the county seat at Tucson for my birth certificate, but they got back to me saying since I didn't know my exact birthday or even my last name, I ought to try Prescott, the territorial capital. Mr. Levy himself was going up there and promised to look into it for me.

It was when Mr. Levy had gone off to Prescott and left me in charge of the store that things got a little out of hand. It was the early evening, and Rebecca was helping me close things up, when I heard loud voices and a few gunshots and broken bottles coming out of the saloon.

"Wilsons," I said to Rebecca. "Whyn't you go into the house, darlin'?" It was the first time I ever called her that, and I liked the way it sounded. I think she did, too.

"I'm not afraid of that trash," she said.

"Yeah, well, I am," I said to her. "And Jake's out at the mine seeing Lida Mae. Damn!"

Rebecca picked up the six-gun her father had given me from under the counter. "Let 'em come," she said.

"Becky! Put that down!"

"I know how to use it. Papa taught me."

"You're not shootin' anybody. Now, go on, git outta here!"

"I'll go get help, then," she said.

"Fine," I said, eager to get her out of there. "Git! Not that way! Out the back!"

I practically shoved her out the back door just as the Wilsons was coming in the front. Tad was in front, like usual.

He had a big smile on his face, which made him even scarier. "Why, hello, Nate," he said, sweet as pie. He looked around the store. "Seems you done come up in the world."

"Just tryin' to make a living," I said.

The other Wilsons was just standing there, not doing

nothing. Then Virge picked up a music box and stuck it in his coat.

"Put that back," I said, trying to keep my voice from shaking.

"Who's gon' make me?" Virge asked. I noticed his nose was a little flat from where I'd slogged him. Good.

"Virge!" Tad cautioned him, shaking his head. Virge tssked and put the music box back where he'd found it. "So, is Aaron about?" Tad asked.

"He's away for a bit," I said.

"And Jake?"

"The same."

"Well, now, ain't that a shame. And here we done rode all the way into town for nothing."

"Oh, well," I said, "mebbe next time. Have a nice ride back to the ranch, fellers," I added, hoping they'd take the hint. A course, they didn't. Tad sat down at the stove and stretched a bit. I looked uneasily at the six-gun beneath the counter. I'd been practicing, but Tad was still the fastest gun in town, except for Jake.

"Was you gonna buy something, Tad?" I asked.

"You wouldn't be tryna git rid a us, now wouldya, Nate?"

"Uh, no, it's just that I got a lotta work to do, and if there's nothin'—"

"Election's day after tomorrow, Nate," Tad said. "Looks like I'm gon' be the new marshal round here. You might wanna be friends with me."

"Oh? And how would I go about that?"

"What's old Jake got up his sleeve?" Tad asked. "He ain't doin' nothing about this here election. I know Aaron went up Prescott way. What for?"

"Don't know," I said.

"Come on, Nate. You don't want to get on the wrong side of the law, now, do you?"

"I don't think that'll be a problem for me," I said, finally tired of him and his no-good brothers, "since I'll be on the stage outta here five minutes after you pin on your badge."

Tad had been leaning back in the chair and now sat forward with a bang. "That ain't neighborly—not at all. You need a lesson in manners."

"Not from you," I said. I did some fast figuring. There was three Wilsons between me and the front door. I wasn't counting Virge.

"Boys?" Tad said. "Not you, Earl. Fair's fair." Bob and Buck began walking toward me. I felt under the counter for the truncheon Mr. Levy kept there. The two of them came behind the counter, one on each side, with me in the middle. I quick grabbed the truncheon and swung out, hitting Buck just below the jaw and knocking him backward. Then I rounded on Bob and found myself staring into the barrel of a six-gun. Bob had this crazy smile on his face as he pulled back the hammer and cocked the gun.

"I'd put that away if I was you," came a deep voice from the front of the store. Earl turned around right quick but was conked on the head with the butt of a Colt .45. A Peacemaker with a seven-and-a-half-inch barrel, I noticed, although I don't know why I bothered when I had other things to think about.

Anyhow, Earl went down with a crash like to knock over the shelves.

"I said put that away," the voice said.

"Who the hell are you?" Bob demanded.

The stranger stepped into the store. He was tall, with

dark blond hair and a big handlebar mustache, sort of like Jake's.

Tad, who had stood up and was about to draw down, closed his eyes and whispered, "Oh, shit."

"What?" Bob wanted to know.

"Put away the gun, Bob," Tad said. "Just do what I say."

"That's good advice," the stranger said. "Now, all a you, git the hell outta here, afore I git mad."

A very beautiful, finely dressed, dark-haired woman swept into the store, stepping lightly over Earl's still form.

"Honestly!" The woman scolded the stranger. "I can't take you anywhere! When are you going to learn to play nice?"

"Sorry, honey," the man said with a grin. "You know how I get when I see a lotta men with guns pickin' on someone who ain't got one."

"Well, I forgive you." The woman came up to me, completely ignoring the Wilsons. "Have you any perfume in this establishment, young man?"

Well, that was a new one on me. I had Bob Wilson holding a gun on me on one side, Buck Wilson bleeding on the floor on the other, Earl Wilson out cold in front, Virge Wilson about to pee himself, and Tad Wilson looking more afeared than I'd ever seen him—and a lady was asking me about toilet water. And I thought nothing could happen in Arizona that would surprise me.

The stranger turned to Tad. "You. With the insane-asylum eyes. You get this menagerie outta here. And tell that feller with the gun he's got a last chance to put it away before I stick it up his ass."

"Oh, you!" the pretty woman gushed. "You've been into my poetry books again, haven't you?"

I'd been learning a lot about men and women lately, and here was another interesting thing. This feller was obviously a tough customer who didn't laugh much, but this woman had him wrapped around her pinky finger. It was maybe the first time I'd ever seen a couple that much in love—not like the first few days when you feel like there's a balloon in your head, but much later, when you're used to each other and find that you're still over the moon, anyhow.

It was just then that Tad decided to be brave. "Look here," he said, trying to be stern but his voice quivering a little, "I'm the law around here."

"You are?" the stranger asked. "Where's your badge?"

"Uh . . . well, I ain't got one yet. But I'll be elected day after tomorrow."

"Is that a fact?" The stranger pulled back his coat to show a U.S. deputy marshal's badge. "Well, I'm the law here now, and I say get outta here. And you," he said to Bob, "you still ain't put that damn gun away."

Bob holstered real quick. The Wilsons didn't leave right away, because they had some heavy lifting to do. First they had to drag Earl outside, and with his blubber, that took awhile. Then they had to come back and help Buck. I guess I'd messed up his jaw just a bit. Finally, they was all gone, and I was able to breathe a little.

"That was a hell of a job, son," the man said. "Standing up to five armed men like that. Looks like that one feller's gonna be drinking his meals for awhile. You got guts, boy."

"Thank you, sir. I was plenty scared, though."

"Be a fool if you wasn't. This Mr. Aaron Levy's shop?"

"Yes, sir. I'm—"

"Nathaniel. Is that right?"

"Yes, sir," I said, surprised.

"Ran into Mr. Levy on the way to Prescott," he said. "He asked the governor if he'd send someone to oversee your election, make sure it all went off fair. I got the job."

"He did?" I sighed with relief. So that was why Aaron had gone up to Prescott. A good thing, too. Maybe the election wouldn't be all sewed up for Tad, after all.

"Well, I'm sure glad you're here," I said. "Whoever you are, you're welcome."

The man smiled. "I'm sorry. I thought Mr. Levy'd sent word. I'm Wyatt Earp," he said. "Oh—and this is my . . . fiancée, Josie."

Wyatt Earp! No wonder Tad had been so scared. Wyatt was pretty famous throughout Arizona, as you may have suspected. He had just left Tombstone after his kid brother Morgan had been killed and his older brother Virgil had been shot through his shoulder and lost the use of his left arm. Virgil was on his way to California, and as it would turn out, Wyatt would soon take his revenge on the men who had killed Morgan. But, for a few days, at least, he would be part of our town, and we were damned glad to have him.

"Mr. Earp, Miss Josie," I said, "I'm awful glad to meet you. Can I direct you to the hotel?"

"We'll find it all right, son," Wyatt said. "Is the town marshal about?"

"He's right here," said Jake, who had suddenly appeared in the doorway. "I'm Jake Murchison."

Wyatt touched the brim of his hat. "Wyatt Earp, Marshal. And this here's Miss Josie Marcus."

"Had the pleasure of seeing Miss Josie onstage awhile back in Tucson," Jake said. "I wonder if you might both be my guests for supper at the hotel."

"That's right kindly of you, Marshal."

"If you gentlemen will excuse me," Miss Josie said, "I must freshen up if we're to be the marshal's guests. That is the hotel across the street?"

"Yes, ma'am," I said. "I'll walk you there if—"

"Oh, that's quite all right, young man. I've been crossing streets alone for some time now. I'll check us in, Wyatt."

When she had gone, I turned my attention to Jake and Wyatt. They were so much alike in looks and in aspect, it made me wonder how well they'd get along. I found out soon enough: They didn't.

"Mr. Earp, a word before you go to the hotel."

"Marshal."

He walked Earp out the door, I guess for privacy. But I heard them anyway.

"Mr. Earp, your reputation precedes you, as I'm sure you must know. Exactly what is your brief here?"

"I understand your concern, Marshal. In Tombstone, and even in Dodge, there was often an overlapping of jurisdictions. The town police, the county sheriff, the U.S. marshals. The trouble with the West, in my humble opinion, is not that there are too few lawmen, but too many.

"In answer to your question, I am a deputy U.S. marshal charged with overseeing your elections tomorrow. When your ballots have been counted and the marshal has been sworn in, I will have earned my hundred-dollar fee and will leave your fair city. Is that good enough?"

"Perhaps," Jake said. "I heard of your recent tragedy. I'm very sorry for your loss."

Wyatt didn't say nothing to that; he just nodded.

"However—" Jake continued.

"I know what you're getting at, Murchison," Wyatt

said. He was getting a little riled, but he was trying hard
not to show it.

"Do you?"

"I do. You want to know if the surviving members of
the Clanton gang will be riding through with their guns
blazing, is that it?"

"Yes, that is it, Mr. Earp. I have enough on my plate
here as it is. I do not need Tombstone's violence spreading here into Granger. I will not allow any OK Corrals in
this town."

"Do you really think I would let that happen?"

"I don't know, Mr. Earp. You see, sir, as marshal of
this town, my concern is upholding the law and protecting
the citizens—and nothing else. I'm not here to get rich;
I'm not fighting for economic control of this town. Because I believe that law enforcement is a full-time job
with no room for conflicts of interest."

I didn't hear Wyatt's answer to that, but I could tell he
was stung. Jake had pretty much slapped him in the face,
same as saying, "I'm a lawman and I'm honest. You were
a lawman and you also ran a gambling hall and wanted
as much money as you could pull out of Tombstone, any
way you could."

"So," Earp said in a low voice that would have terrified
a lesser man, "you think you're better than me, is that it?"

But Jake wasn't a lesser man. "Better?" he said. "No.
But let's just say I'm more sure of my mission as a peace
officer than you are."

I could bet that Wyatt's cheeks were probably blazing
red by now. "I think this discussion is at an end. And I
think my fiancée and I will dine elsewhere tonight."

"That's your privilege," Jake said. "I'll see you in the
morning at the polling place."

"I don't see how I can avoid that," Wyatt said and was gone.

I walked outside and saw Jake watching his new enemy cross the street.

"I sure handled that well, didn't I, Nathaniel?" Jake said cheerfully.

"Jake. What in *the* hell did you do that for? Why would you want Wyatt Earp mad at you?"

"Because he knows I'm right," Jake replied. "He's a good man at the bottom—but it's at the bottom. Now he's going to go out of his way to prove me wrong, to prove he's a good cop. And that's the way I want it, for as long as he wears a badge in my town."

I shook my head admiringly. "You figured all that out, just like that? What if you'd been wrong?"

"If I had been wrong, then neither one of us should have been wearing a badge."

10

ELECTION DAY DAWNED bright, sunny, and damned hot, which meant that everyone would turn out for it, if only to find a way to take their minds off the heat. I woke up early and met Jake for breakfast in the dining room. He told me that Marshal Earp was already at the polling place, where he and Judge Hackett were setting things up.

There was a sheaf of papers about half a foot high next to Jake's plate of waffles.

"What's that?" I asked him as he skimmed through it.

"The judge's book," he said, not looking up from the pages. "It's not bad at all, and better than I expected."

"He really done finished it?" I asked him.

"It would seem so. I suppose my cousin at Columbia College just might find this interesting. He does—"

"Gentlemen? May I join you?"

We both stood up. "Morning, Miss Josie," I said.

"Ma'am," Jake said. "Won't you sit down?"

"Thank you," she replied. She looked over at Jake's

reading material. "I'm not intruding, am I?"

"No, ma'am, not at all."

"Hmmmm," she said, glancing at a page. " 'The Restoration comedy treats the cuckold with a particularly brutal contempt. Perhaps this is as it should be, for it accurately reflects the social conditions of the time. But it does beg the question: Is the cuckold an object of humor merely because he is cuckolded? Where is the true humor in infidelity? Or is our laughter more viscerally motivated, perhaps out of a sense of relief?' This is marvelous. Are you the author, Marshal?"

"No, Miss Josie, it's our town magistrate, Judge Hackett."

"I think I should like to meet him," she said.

"I can arrange that. He'll be working with Mr. Earp today."

The waiter brought Miss Josie a cup of coffee. "I have a bone to pick with you, Marshal," she said.

"Pick away, ma'am."

"I think you treated Wyatt rather abominably yesterday."

"I'm sure you're right."

"You are? Then why did you do it?"

"I have strong views about a policeman's duty, Miss Marcus. I am aware that in Tombstone things may well have been different. For example, I understand that your county sheriff—"

"Not *my* county sheriff. I've had all of Cochise County I can stomach."

"Nevertheless, in that county, the law is a highly profitable calling. It's a matter of record that Sheriff Behan, as tax collector, has netted for himself well over thirty

thousand dollars so far this year. And that Mr. Earp himself made plenty of money running a faro game while
serving as town marshal."

"*Assistant* marshal," she corrected him. "A job he never
wanted, but his brothers Virgil and Morgan needed his
help. Could you refuse your brothers?"

"I have no brothers. But I do have a badge. And while
I wear that badge, I cannot serve two masters, only one:
the law."

"And from what I understand about this town, when
the polls close today, you will still be serving the law, for
which you will have Wyatt to thank."

"And I will. As Wyatt would have me to thank if he
ever needed my help in upholding the law."

Miss Josie looked at Jake as if to see right through him.
"You're a zealot, Marshal."

"Maybe I am. But the law deserves a zealot if it gets
the job done and keeps people safe. And, if it makes any
difference to you, I didn't seek this job, either."

She smiled. She had a killer grin, all right. "I admire
your strength of character, Marshal. But I do hope you'll
go a bit easier on mere mortals like me . . . and Wyatt. He
hasn't had an easy time of it."

"I'll do my best, ma'am. Mr. Earp is fortunate to have
someone like you pleading his case."

"He's a good man, Marshal. Give him a chance."

"I might as well," Jake said. "We might all be requiring
his protection at the end of the day."

The ballot boxes were set up in the Wells Fargo office.
Wyatt and Judge Hackett sat at a table with a register for
each voter to sign. The voting itself was pretty simple;

one box for Jake and the other for Tad Wilson. I left Rebecca in charge of the store and walked over to see how things were going. I passed by Jake, who was sitting in his usual spot outside his office.

"Jake," I said, "ain't you gonna at least get out there? Shake a few hands?"

"What for? Everybody knows me by now."

I couldn't say nothing to that, so I walked on ahead.

The Wilsons had set up a free lunch and free beer table in front of Tom Tryer's saloon. All the Wilsons were there, even old Alvin. They was all shaking fellers' hands, acting all friendly-like. I wondered if anyone was fooled. I also wondered what-all they had up their sleeve. They couldn't bully nobody, not with Wyatt and Jake around. So I watched real close, and soon I got it.

"A vote for my boy is a vote for law and order," I heard Alvin say as he shook a feller's hand. The feller got a surprised look on his face and then looked at his palm, which now had a silver dollar in it.

Well, I run just as fast as ever I could for the voting room.

"Judge! Judge Hackett!"

"Well, young Nathaniel! What can I do for you, my boy?"

"I think we got a problem, Judge." He listened as I told him what I'd seen.

"Sounds like they're buying votes," Wyatt said. "You want me to go out there and see what I can do, Judge?"

"Thank you, Mr. Earp. But we have a legal issue here. There's nothing wrong with giving a man a dollar. We can't prosecute them for generosity. And we can't prove that the dollar is for a vote."

"Maybe," Wyatt said. "But I can sure make 'em stop."

"I'm sure you can, Mr. Earp. But on what legal grounds?"

"Well, sir, you're the judge around here. You oughta know the law better'n anybody else. They must be violatin' *somethin'.*"

The judge put his hands together and closed his eyes, almost like he was praying. "Let me think . . . free lunch—no, law's there; beer . . . no, it could be considered an extension of the saloon . . . damn it! This is what happens when you go for six weeks without a drink!"

I was flabbergasted. "Judge? You been dry six weeks?"

"Of course I have! How in God's name do you think I've been able to finish writing my book? You can thank Irma for that!"

"I think she's the best thing ever happened to you, Judge."

"Yes, and she always tells me so, adding, however, that I am not necessarily the best thing that's ever happened to *her.*"

Wyatt broke out of his somber look with a quick chuckle. "She sounds too good to be true, this Irma."

"That she is, and now will the both of you kindly shut up so that I may consider—" The judge stopped talking suddenly and stood up. "Mr. Earp? Will you accompany me, please?"

"Be glad to, Judge."

I didn't want to miss this, so I helped Wyatt stow the ballot boxes behind the Wells Fargo counter and followed them down the street. Jake saw where we were headed and made his way toward us.

Most of the fellers in front of the saloon were there for the beer. Nobody seemed in any hurry to go and vote. I think they was afraid that once they actually voted, the Wilsons might have no more use for them and stop giving away the free stuff, so they was loading up while they could.

"Now, you all remember who to vote for," Tad was saying.

"Yeah, 'member who gave y'all this free stuff," Earl said, eating a chicken leg.

"Save some for the boys, there, Earl," Alvin Wilson said. "Cecil," he called to the judge. "Have a beer."

"I'm sorry, Alvin, but I'm here in an official capacity."

"An official capacity," Wilson said. "And for what purpose might that be?"

"I'm sorry, but you gentlemen are in violation of local and territorial ordinances against electioneering."

"What the hell are you talking about, Judge?" Tad demanded.

"Shut up," Wyatt said.

"Can I be of any assistance here?" Jake asked.

Wyatt turned to Jake. "Marshal, this is an election issue. My jurisdiction. Thank you, but I'll handle this."

Jake regarded him carefully and then nodded. "Very well, Marshal. You know where to find me if you change your mind." He turned on his heel and walked away.

"Cecil!" Alvin said angrily. "You can't do this!"

"I'm sorry, Alvin. The law is the law. This entire setup must be moved—Marshal?"

"I can pace off a thousand feet if you like, Judge. But I'd say it's that clump a trees yonder."

"Good enough. Gentlemen?"

"I'll get you for this, you old drunk!" Tad seethed.

That got Wyatt's attention. He pointed to Tad. "You. Get over here."

"What for?"

I started to laugh. I couldn't help it. Why would anyone challenge Wyatt Earp like that?

"Is something funny, young man?" Alvin asked me.

"I'll let you know in a minute," I said.

Wyatt glared at Tad, who shuffled over to him like a little kid.

"Did I hear right? Did I just hear you threaten a public official?"

" 'S a free country," Tad said. "I can say whatever—"

Wyatt grabbed Tad and pinned his arms behind him. "That's enough. You're goin' to jail."

"Technically," the judge said, as if he was a tutor explaining the multiplication table, "you can't say *whatever* if it constitutes any sort of a threat. I'm telling you this, Tad, because as an aspiring lawman, you ought to be conversant with this sort of thing. Legally, that is known as assault, and Mr. Earp is within his rights if he does choose to place you in custody. However, Mr. Earp, I'd rather you didn't at this time."

Wyatt shoved Tad away. "Let me know if you change your mind, Judge. Now, all of you; I'll be back here in fifteen minutes, and this whole damn picnic better not be here."

"Be seein' ya, Judge," Tad said ominously. Wyatt turned on him quickly, but Tad put up his hands like he didn't mean nothin' by it. "I just said, 'Be seein' ya,' that's all."

"Come along, Mr. Earp," the judge said. "We've got a long day ahead."

It was a long day. At the end of it, Jake was elected town marshal by a ten-to-one vote. But our celebrating was short-lived. The night ahead would be even longer.

11

THE BALLOTS WEREN'T near half counted when it become pretty clear that Jake would win in a walk. I tried to go back to the store and get some work done on the inventory, but I kept making excuses to go back to the Wells Fargo office, and finally Rebecca just laughed and kicked me out for good.

They was almost finished counting up the ballots when the late stage pulled in, and Aaron Levy got out.

"Aaron!" I shouted. "You done it! Was your idea all along to bring in Mr. Earp! Well, sir, it worked! It worked! Jake's won it by a mile!"

"That's fine, Nathaniel," he said, but he didn't look too happy. Not about Jake's winning, but like he'd heard bad news about something else.

"Aaron? Are you all right? What's the matter?"

"Let's go over to the store, Nathaniel."

"What's wrong?" I asked, real frightened now.

Aaron walked slower than usual, like whatever was on his mind was like an anvil on his shoulders. When we got to the store, he kissed Becky hello, and she could right away tell something was wrong.

"Papa? What is it?"

"I need to talk to Nathaniel, sweetheart."

My heart beat hard like it always did when I was real scared. I quick thought something might of happened out at the mine.

"Is Ned all right?" I asked. "Lida Mae? Emlyn?"

"I wouldn't know," Aaron said. "I haven't been anywhere near the mine. No, this is about . . . you. Rebecca?"

"She's part of whatever happens to me, Aaron," I said. "She stays."

"Very well," Aaron said. "Nate, I want you to know, you've been like a son to me. No matter what, I'll never change my mind about that. I think you're better than the rest of us, and I'll always think that."

Becky grabbed my arm. "Papa? What is it?"

Aaron's eyes were wet; there was no mistaking it as he dug into his pocket and came out with an official-looking piece of paper. I saw the words "Certification of Birth" and knew right away that nothing on that document was going to make me feel very good.

I was able to read that I was born in Tucson on March 3, 1866. But by the time I got to the line that said "mother" and "father," my tears had already blurred my eyesight.

"Nate?" Rebecca said fearfully. I slid down onto the floor and held up the paper so that Rebecca could read it.

"Oh, Nate!" she cried and fell down next to me. She was crying and kissing me at the same time. "I love you, Nate! It doesn't matter! I love you! I'll always love you!"

In one tiny part of my brain, I figured myself damn lucky to have a girl like Rebecca. But the rest of me was on fire. I was sad, hurt, humiliated, a whole bunch of things. And still Becky was holding me and telling me she loved me.

Finally, I couldn't take no more. I gently removed myself from Rebecca's embrace. Then I got up and went screaming out the door.

I heard Aaron call behind me. "Nate! Nate! Wait! Jake! Jake, you there!"

"What is it, Aaron?"

"Nate! Go!"

But by then I was charging through the door of Tom Tryer's saloon. Ike Hawkins stood in front of me, blocking my way.

"What do you want? You're not welcome in here."

"You'd best git outta my way," I growled.

"Or else, what?"

I didn't wait to think up no answer; I just kicked him hard as I could right in the willies and pushed past him as he crumpled onto the floor. I made my way over to the joyhouse door and two apes come running.

"Get outta my way, apes," I said.

"Turn around and go," one of them said, "and none a your bones'll get broken."

"Move away from the door," I heard Jake's voice say. "Do it now."

That left the apes with little choice but to do what he said. I pushed through the door and saw Miss Flora, who had come in to see what the fuss was about.

"Nate?" she asked with a surprised look on her face. "What is the meaning of this?"

I grabbed her hand and slapped the paper into it. "I don't know. Why don't you tell me the meaning of *this! Mother!*"

Miss Flora—or should I say, *Mama*—collapsed into a chair and began to weep. Like most men, I'm a sucker for a woman's tears, and all my anger started melting away. At first. Then I remembered all the years of sweeping up and changing dirty sheets and wet towels in my ear and living in the barn while she was right there, *my own mother,* not fifty feet away, not a kiss, not a hug, not a care! And before I knew it, I was mad as hell again.

"Why'd you do it, Flora?" I demanded. "What the hell kind of person are you? I'm almost growed up now, so you c'n go to hell for all I need you, but I was a little baby once! And you was right there all along!"

"Nate," she wept, "you don't understand—"

"You're damn right I don't understand. Was I ugly? Was I sick? Was I slow in the head? What'd I do?"

"It wasn't you, Nate! It was me. I couldn't—"

"You couldn't what?" I ignored the tears that were starting to pour from my eyes. "You couldn't hold me in your arms? You couldn't tuck me in and kiss me good night? You couldn't put your hand to my head and say, 'Nate, are you feeling poorly?' You couldn't send me to school so I'd . . . I'd have some *friends?*"

"It's all right for you to hate me, Nate. I don't blame you one—"

"I don't want to hate my own mother, goddamn it!"

"Nate . . ."

I snatched the birth certificate out of her hands. "I don't know what the hell I'm supposed to do now."

"Why don't you come along with me, Nate," Jake said, speaking for the first time. "Nothing has to be decided now."

"Decided? Shit!" I said miserably. I turned back to Flora. "And you know what the funniest thing of all is?

The funniest damn thing is that I always liked you, Flora. I even—and here's the real hoot—I even thought, *That Miss Flora's such a fine, sweet woman, I wouldn't mind it at all if she was my mother!"*

Flora sort of hiccupped and put her hand to her face and then started crying for real, almost like a kid who fell off a pony.

"I think we're all through here for now, Nathaniel," Jake whispered to me.

"I guess you're right, Jake. But you haven't heard the good part yet."

"The good part?"

"Oh, yeah, Jake, the good part. Seems I come from really fine stock. Wait'll you hear who my goddamn *father* is!"

"You'll tell me when you're ready," he said, leading me out the door. I didn't look back.

Tom Tryer met us at the door. "What's goin' on in here?" he demanded. "This little bastard done assaulted my bartender." He pointed to where Ike was still doubled over on the floor.

Jake turned and threw Tom up against the wall.

"All right, Mickey, I've heard about enough from you." He banged Tom's head against the wall. "How long's it been since anyone called you by that name . . . *Mickey?* Corporal Michael Hillard, of the U.S. Fifth Cavalry?"

"Is that right," I remarked.

"Isn't that right, *Mickey?"* Jake said, tightening his hand on Tom's throat. "You might want to know, *Mickey,* that there's a deputy U.S. marshal in town. What if I were to tell him that I have here the Corporal Hillard who stole the regimental payroll and went missing with it? I guess that's how you bought your way into this dump, huh,

Mickey? What if I told him you ruined a promising officer's career with that little trick?

"Oh, nobody blamed me, Mickey. But it was *on my watch,* you little turd!" That was the first time I ever saw Jake lose his temper, and for a minute I was scared. The veins stood out on his neck, and his face went all red. Tom—or Mickey, I guess I should say—looked frightened enough to be facing the hangman himself. Then I saw Jake fight to get control.

"It went on my record, Mickey," he said in a calmer voice, "and when I wasn't promoted first lieutenant along with the rest of my academy class, I took the hint and went home."

"I didn't mean to hurt you, Lieutenant," Tom said. "Honest I didn't! I didn't know it'd get you in trouble!"

Jake let him go, his hands flying off of Tom like he was covered in horse dung. "Let's get out of here, Nathaniel. We'd best hurry, before one of us hurts someone."

Jake put his arm across my shoulders as we crossed the street. "I'd offer you a drink if you weren't too young, Nathaniel. It seems as though you need one."

"I'll settle for a cup of that rotten coffee of yours, Jake," I said. It was funny, but my . . . misfortune, I guess you could call it, had made me feel more like Jake's equal than some kid who scampered around after him like a puppy dog. I think Jake understood that, too, because he acted a bit different around me, more like a friend than a grown-up interested in my welfare.

We went into his office. "You know, Jake, I'm sorry. I forgot to congratulate you on whuppin' Tad's butt today."

He waved it off. "It's nothing. I didn't win; the town just protected its own interests. It's Judge Hackett and

Marshal Earp who deserve the credit. I was wrong about
him. I owe him an apology."

"I'm sure you'll get the chance. And I'm sorry about
your army career. Maybe you'd be a general by now."

He laughed and swung his feet onto his desk. "You
know, Nate, in a way, I really wasn't fair to old Mickey.
If you want to know the truth, he did me a favor—that
is, the man I am now, not the boy I was eight years ago."

I didn't get it. "How do you mean?"

"Well, every shavetail gets out of West Point champing
at the bit, craving action. When I graduated from the
Point, every one of us was spitting nails because we
missed the war, missed our chances for glory and quick
promotion. What fools we were! After the war, what was
left for a cavalryman? A dull, stultifying life on a barren
post. General! I'd have been lucky to be a major after
thirty years!" He smiled sadly. "But I didn't know that
then—and if I did, I never would have accepted it."

We heard a horse gallop in and slow to a trot, then stop
in front of Jake's office. The rider dismounted, and I
looked out the window and saw that it was Lida Mae.

She hurried inside. Jake stood up, and she rushed into
his arms. "Oh, you won, you won! I'm so happy!" She
turned her face up and kissed him. It was the first time I
ever saw them kiss, and I realized Jake was maybe gone
over her, but she was plum silly over him. *Well, why not?*
I thought. *Everybody deserves the right to be happy.*

"Oh, hello, Nate," she said, noticing me for the first
time.

"Oh, hey," I said. "Why don't I just leave the two a
you—"

"It's all right, Nate," she said, and her voice had changed
into the businesslike tone that I had come to know well,

the one that struck fear in the hearts of every vendor who came anywhere near the mining camp. "There's something Daddy asked me to speak to you about."

"Let's all get comfortable, then," Jake said, pulling out a chair for her. "Will you be staying in town tonight?"

She looked him square in the eye. "Yes, I think I'll seek accommodations at the hotel this evening. I would like a bath, to begin with."

I looked up at the ceiling and tried hard not to smile.

She cleared her throat and said, "Nate, Daddy has a favor to ask of you."

"Whatever he wants," I said.

"You might not like this," she warned me.

"I'm sure I will."

"We'll see. Nate, Daddy's not sure how much longer the mine will be paying out."

"What do you mean?"

"Well, I don't know much about it, but Daddy does, and so does Emlyn Jones. Maybe you've heard of the way mines work in Arizona. Sometimes a mine will produce for years. Sometimes it'll look good at first, pay out a fortune, then nothing. And then, it might pay out, then look like it's finished, but it'll turn out there's an even bigger lode beneath it."

I shrugged. "I figured as much. So?"

"Well, the point is, there's no way to be sure. And Emlyn and his boys risked a lot to come in with us. If the mine goes bust tomorrow, they'll have nowhere to go. They obviously can't go back to work for Wilson."

"No," I replied thoughtfully, "they can't do that."

"Well, Daddy was thinking, they're all good men, maybe we ought to give them shares in the profits, like Fred and Whitetail."

"Sure," I said. "Fine with me. They're the reason there's profits to begin with. You want to make 'em stockholders in the mine. Is that it?"

"You're sure it's all right with you?"

"If they have a stake in the place, it's better all around, ain't it? They wouldn't just be workin' for us, but for themselves, too."

"You're a good businessman, Nate," she said approvingly.

"I know," I said tiredly. "It's a talent I got from my mother."

Jake choked on his coffee.

"Jake?" Lida Mae said. "you all right?"

There was a sudden commotion outside. "Marshal! Marshal! You in there, Marshal?"

"Come on in," Jake called.

It was Jimmy Bell, the cook over at Zeb Stanton's. He was possibly the skinniest feller in Arizona, could damn near fit through a keyhole. You wouldn't expect somebody who looked like that to be the best cook in the county, but he was. I've heard folks talk about Paris, France, but old Jimmy could show 'em a thing or two.

"Jimmy, what can I do for you?"

You could almost see through Jimmy's pale face. "You'd best git over to the judge's house, Marshal," Jimmy said.

"What happened?" Jake said, getting up quickly.

"I was bringin' 'im dinner. He likes my steaks, see. I went to knock on the door, but it was a little opened. Somebody done shot him," Jimmy said in a rush, "him and Irma. Please git over there, Marshal."

"Oh, Lord," I said. "I'm a-comin' with you, Jake."

Jake stopped for a second like he was gonna say no but

then changed his mind. "All right," he said. "Jimmy, go fetch Doc Hayes. Have him meet me at the judge's."

"He ain't gonna need no doctor," Jimmy said.

"Just do it. Then go back to the hotel and get Marshal Earp. Oh, and is there anyone in town with a camera?"

"What do you need a camera for?" I asked him. He shook his head at me, same as saying, "Not now."

"There's a feller stayin' at the hotel, passin' through," Jimmy said.

"Then get him, too. And, Jimmy? Did you touch anything?"

"No, sir! But—well, I dropped the dinner'n ran. Made a mess, I bet."

"It's all right. You did fine." He picked up a pad and pencil and thrust it at me. "You want to help, Nate? Then you do exactly as I say. Understand?"

"Yes, sir," I said. "Jake? You think you know who did it?"

"I'm pretty sure," he said. "But proving it is going to be something else again.

12

DOC HAYES WAS delivering a baby, so he couldn't meet us right away. That turned out to be all right, though, because the photographer took such a long time with the pictures.

It was a horrifying scene. They was in the judge's study, on this big old Chesterfield couch he had in there. The judge was sitting down with his head thrown back and his eyes open, a ragged, bloody hole in his forehead. Irma lay across his lap. There was blood all over the place, though most of it was dry and turning brown by now. What got me was that you couldn't tell whose blood was whose, the judge's or Irma's.

There was something not entirely real about it. It was almost like, for a second, like they was kidding. Like you could say, "Okay, Judge, Irma, very funny, you can git up now." Only, they wouldn't.

The photographer, a big, heavy guy name of Syms with a derby hat and one of those salesman-type checkered suits, scratched his head and wanted to know why Jake needed pictures. So did I, but I was glad somebody else asked.

"Because I don't want to have to rely on my memory when I'm trying to figure out exactly how they were killed. A lot of big-city police forces are starting to use photographers now," Jake said.

"Yeah, well, who's going to pay the bill?" Syms said. "That's what I want to know."

Jake rolled his eyes and took some money out of his pocket. "Here," he told Syms, "now, get started. I want pictures of the whole room and the bodies from every angle."

"That'll take some time, Marshal."

"Then don't waste any arguing with me. Wyatt, thanks for getting here so quickly."

"Sure," Wyatt said, slightly surprised at Jake's use of his first name. I guess he figured that was Jake's way of apologizing. "What've we got?"

"The judge and his housekeeper. Shot dead, looks like six shots, five hits."

Wyatt nodded. "Emptied his gun at them, I reckon. You figurin' what I'm figurin'?"

"It's likely," Jake nodded.

"It's more'n likely. I heard him threaten the judge today when we broke up that picnic. I was gonna take him in, but the judge told me not to. Damn it! I shouldn't a listened to him. He'd be alive right now."

"It's not your fault," Jake said. "You couldn't have known. Come on, let's step outside while the photographer does his bit."

We went outside onto the judge's porch. Wyatt offered Jake a cigar and lit it for him, and we just stood there and waited.

"It sounds stupid now," I said to Jake, "but I'm sure glad he finished that book of his."

"It's not so stupid, Nate," Jake said. "I'm glad, too." He turned to Wyatt. "I've got a slight legal problem," he said. "I'm going to need a search warrant, but I don't have the time to find another judge. You're an experienced territorial lawman. Any suggestions?"

"Will the judge have any blank warrants around?"

"I would think so," Jake said.

"Then here's what I would do. Declare a civic emergency and enact martial law. Then use your temporary powers to appoint a new judge. Your mayor, Mr. Levy, would seem the right fellow for the job."

Jake nodded. "Good thinking. But if it comes down to it, will a warrant signed by a temporary judge be admissible in court?"

Wyatt gave him a slow grin. "Something tells me it won't matter if you find what you're lookin' for."

"Good thinking, Marshal, well done."

Syms came out of the house, lugging his camera and equipment and sweating like a tired horse. "All through here, Marshal," he said.

"I want those developed now," Jake said.

"I only got two hands, Marshal."

"Then use them both. Nate: First, I want you to write down the time that Jimmy reported this incident. Then write down what we got here. Next, I want the names of everyone who's been in this room. Start with Jimmy, then us, then the photographer. Anybody comes in or goes out, write it down and the time. Okay, we've got this mess of plates and food that Jimmy dropped here at the threshold. The doorjamb is splintered; probably the killer kicked it in. Write it down. And then write down everything any-body says. Can you handle that?"

"I'm pretty sure I can," I said.

"Good. Let's go in. Careful, don't step on that mess, and nobody touch anything. Wyatt, any thoughts at all, don't be bashful about letting us in on them."

"I been called lots a things in my life," Wyatt said, "but bashful ain't never been one a them."

"Good." Jake stopped suddenly and looked down at the floor. "Bottle of whiskey on the floor, some left in the bottle, not enough to spill out. We are directly across from the victims."

"So the killer," Wyatt said, "was probably drunk and taunting the victim first. Am I right? Unless the judge was drinking and threw the bottle at the killer."

"No," Jake said. "Look at the end table next to the Chesterfield. There's a cup of coffee, half-finished."

"The judge said he hadn't drunk nothing in six weeks," I told Jake.

"That's right," Wyatt said, "I remember him mention-ing that."

"Write it down," Jake said. "Doc, glad you're here."

Doc Hayes stepped carefully into the room. He was in his shirtsleeves and looked exhausted. "Difficult birth," he said. "But mother and son are doing fine. And now two deaths." He shook his head sadly. The judge had been a good friend of his. "May I examine the bodies, Marshal?"

"By all means. But please tell us everything you see. Nate? Are you up to this?"

Truthfully, I was ready to vomit. The scene was too much, and the dead people were too close to home. They were people I knew and liked, but I had a job to do. Jake was depending on me.

"I'll be fine," I said.

"Go to it, Doc."

Doc Hayes bent over the two bodies. "We have two victims, a Negro woman in her forties and a white man in his early sixties. The woman has been shot twice in the upper left quadrant of the back, and judging from the locations, either wound could be considered mortal. She has also been shot through the left hand, which would appear to be a defensive wound. A fourth shot has barely nicked her left shoulder and could be considered superficial."

"Brave woman," Wyatt said in an almost whisper. "She tried to take the bullets for him."

Doc Hayes turned suddenly. "She was an *exceptional* woman, Marshal," he said with a slight crack in his voice. "Can I move her now?" he asked Jake.

Tears sprang into my eyes, blurring the paper I was writing on. But I ignored it best I could.

"Go ahead."

The doc lifted Irma carefully off of the judge, as if she was a piece of delicate, breakable china. With Irma no longer blocking the view, we could see the judge's chest, which was soaked with blood.

"Christ!" the doc breathed raggedly. "We have . . . excuse me . . . we have, in addition to the fifth shot, which is an instantly mortal wound to the forehead, a sixth shot to the thoracic region, causing major trauma and if not instant, a fairly rapid death."

"Our killer was a fast gun," Jake said, almost like he was teaching school.

"How do you figure?" Wyatt asked. "I'm not disagreein', I just want to know."

"I believe it went like this: The killer was drunk, and he was getting drunker on the judge's whiskey. But it didn't hurt his shooting any. The killer threatened them for awhile, and then got bored and decided the time for talking was over. The first shot hit the judge in the chest. Irma tried to take the shot herself but wasn't fast enough, although she did take the second shot, which was the flesh wound in her shoulder. See the hole in the couch? That's probably where the bullet landed after hitting her. She's thrown herself over the judge, not knowing he's already taken a fatal shot to the chest. The killer tries another shot, but she throws her hand up and takes the round there. The killer puts the next two in her back, either because he's mad at her for getting in the way or else figuring the shots will pass through and hit the judge. The last shot is the one to the judge's head, but they're both dead by then. Doc?"

The doc stood up and wiped his forehead with a handkerchief. "I think that sizes it up pretty well."

"How long do you think they've been dead?"

"An hour, not much more than that."

"It was a fast gun, Jake," Wyatt said, "a very *fast* gun."

"You know anybody that fast?"

Wyatt shook his head. "Only Doc Holliday. Maybe the Ringo Kid. But they're nowhere near these parts, and anyhow, forgettin' Doc's my best friend and the Kid's in Tombstone, they ain't got a motive between them."

"But we *do* know a fast gun with a motive from these parts, don't we?" Jake said.

"Yes, sir," Wyatt replied. "I believe we do. I'll go and find that search warrant now."

"Good. Doc, I guess you can notify the undertaker now."

"Yes," Doc Hayes sighed, "that's what I'll go and do."

"Oh, and Doc, one other thing. I want to post a guard here. Do you know anyone we can trust?"

"They were dear friends, Marshal. I'll stay here tonight. I owe them that much."

Jake put a hand on my shoulder. "Nate? Nate? Are you all right?"

I wasn't. To be honest, I was scared of the way I felt. A cold, hard rage I'd never felt before. Not like I would throw myself at someone and beat them black and blue; but more dangerous—*much* more dangerous. Like I could look a man in the eye, then slowly and carefully pull out a gun and shoot him dead. I didn't like feeling that way, but I couldn't help it. It made me strong.

"Jake," I said in a low voice, "you better deputize me."

"What?" Jake replied.

"You heard me. I'm a-comin' with you."

"Are you serious?"

"Dead serious."

"Nate, I can't—"

"Don't say no, Jake."

"Wyatt, I can't deputize him, can I? He's too young!"

Wyatt was searching through the judge's desk for a warrant. He was doing it slowly, carefully, replacing everything exactly as he found it, out of respect. "I don't know," Wyatt said.

"I weren't too young up at Pima Canyon," I said.

"No," Jake said thoughtfully, "I guess you weren't."

"You know," Wyatt said, "it seems to me that while he's maybe too young to run for marshal—since he ain't old enough to vote—there ain't no law says he can't be a deputy. Least, I don't think there is."

"See?" I argued.

Jake rolled his eyes and sighed. "Raise your right hand," he said. "All right, you're a goddamned deputy. But you're the one who has to square it with Rebecca, not me."

It turned out that I wasn't the only one who wanted to be deputized.

"Why not?" Lida Mae demanded. "Why the hell not?"

"Because I don't want anything to happen to you," Jake said. "And I don't have time to argue with you."

"Then stop arguin' and deputize me! I'm comin' with you, no matter what, so I might as well be a deputy."

"Look, Lida Mae, you're a—"

"A what? A woman?" She gave Jake the kind of smile that any man sees from a woman, he runs and hides, preferably in another state, if he's smart. She gave Jake a shove, and she was surprisingly strong. "Now, you listen to me. You know I can ride. You know *damn* well I can shoot. I'm not going to be sitting home on pins and needles, looking up from my knitting to peer out the window to see if you'll ever be coming back. *I'm going with you.*" She went to the rack on Jake's office wall and picked up a Winchester as easy as another woman might grab a parasol. Then she caught my eye and smiled.

"You see, Nate? We Southern women are very delicate and *very* genteel, but we are not weaklings—and God help the man makes the mistake of believing that!"

"Lida Mae?" Jake said.

"What is it, honey?"

"Raise your right hand and shut up."

As I walked back over to the store to face Rebecca, a voice called to me from the shadows.

"Nate?"

"Who's there?" I said.

Flora Jenks stepped out into the moonlight. "I heard about the judge and Irma," she said.

"Yeah," I said, not really wanting to talk to her. "It's a damn shame. But I don't have time to talk about it right now."

"Nate." She put out her hand to touch my arm but then took it back quickly. "I know I can never make up for . . . what I did . . . or what I didn't do. But—"

I stepped back and put my hands up. "You know what, Flora? Just forget it. Nobody owes me nothin'. It's too late now, anyway."

"Whatever you want. I'll never trouble you, I promise."

" 'S all right. I got nothin' against you, not anymore."

She pulled a document out from her bosom, looked around, and gave it to me.

"What is this?"

"Read it," she said.

I held it up to the moonlight and read it. It gave me the shock of my life, which says a lot, since I had plenty a shocks recently.

"Is this true?" I asked her.

"It's legal and everything. Take it, Nate."

"But this is yours."

"And that also makes it yours."

I held the paper tight in my fist. "I've got to go," I said.

"All right. Nate?"

"What?"

"Can I just . . . do one thing?"

"Sure," I said.

She took a step toward me. Then, slowly, as if I'd dart away if she made a move, she reached out her hand and put it on my forehead, smoothing my hair back. After fifteen and a half years, I had finally felt a mother's touch.

I went into the store to pick up my Colt from behind the counter.

"Nate?" Rebecca said fearfully. I turned around, and she gasped when she saw the badge pinned to my shirt.

"Nate! What have you done? Where are you going?"

"We're going to find the man who killed the judge and Irma." I hitched the gun belt around my waist and felt foolish, like a policeman's kid trying on his father's uniform.

"Aaron? Can I borrow some extra bullets? I might need them. And I'll need your horse."

"I'll saddle her for you," he said. "Nate? I can't stop you, but—"

"It's all right. You know I have to do this."

"Yes," he sighed, "I suppose I do."

I went over and took both of Becky's hands. "You still wanna marry me?" I asked her.

"You know I do. Oh, Nate, please be careful!"

"Time to be careful is over," I said. "Becky, if . . . when I come back, there's something I want you to know about me. I'd a told you before, but I didn't know it myself till just now."

She held me close. "Is it about your parents? I told you before, I don't care about that."

"Neither do I," I said, pushing her out to arms' length. "No. It's about me."

"There's nothing about you I couldn't love," she said.

That made me feel real warm for a second, but I didn't have time to enjoy it. "You might change your mind. Becky, I just found out . . . I grew up too fast. I like what

I've found out about myself since Jake come to town, and how people like him and your folks think highly of me, and that I seem to have a head for business and other growed-up stuff.

"But what I don't like, Becky, is that I ain't never been a kid. I ain't never had a mama bake me a birthday cake, or went to school and dipped a girl's braid in a inkwell, or climbed trees or got a whuppin' for sneakin' strawberry jam outta the pantry. I never had that. I been around folks who get drunk and puke and fight and gamble and take girls upstairs, and then I washed their slimy old bedsheets when they was done."

"It's all right, Nate," she said.

"Well, no, it ain't. I guess I turned out a good kid in spite a all that. Even a smart kid. But, Becky, it ain't enough. I don't care what happens, how much money I ever make. Once things get settled down, I'm gonna try and make up for all the kid-bein' I missed out on. I don't mean I'm gonna do kid things. But I'm gonna try new stuff, I'm gonna . . . explore, with a kid's wonder and without fear. I wanna . . . I wanna ride a hot-air balloon. I wanna visit the ocean and see how far I can swim—if it turns out I can swim. I'll always be like that, Becky. I'll always be a kid with a brand-new toy. Maybe that'll get on your nerves after a while."

"It won't get on my nerves." She took me in her arms and kissed my forehead. "I'll always be there with you. I don't want to miss out on a single kid-smile the second it crosses your face."

13

MANY YEARS LATER, I would get the old raspberry from folks—who asked me in the first place, because I never brought it up myself—when I told them I rode out to find a killer with Wyatt Earp and Gentleman Jake Murchison.

But on that night in 1881, there we was, just like the Four Horsemen you read about—though we was really three horsemen and one horse*woman*. Actually, there was two horsemen. Wyatt was a fine rider, and Jake, of course, had been a cavalry officer, and you can't get much better'n that.

Anybody was better'n me, though. Like I said before, I was tops at saddling horses and washing them down, and I even could shoe 'em in a pinch. But I never had much experience riding them and was never much to holler about as a horseman. I spent much of the time just hanging on for dear life.

But as we rode four abreast through the brush at a fast gallop, sending up big clouds of dust, I guess we was something to see. Especially when we come over a rise, four big shadows made to look colossal as the full moon lit us up from behind. All of us wearing badges; all of us mad as hell; and all of us had killed before. If I'd just been watching us tear on by, and I didn't know it was me, I'd a been scared of us, all right.

The Wilsons' spread was about ten miles south of town. It was a big place, probably the biggest in Arizona. You had to travel a couple more miles to get to old Alvin's house once you was inside his property line. It was a nice place, too. Mrs. Wilson, who died a few years before, had fixed it up real fancy and spent a hell of a lot of Alvin's money doing it.

The place was set back behind a big yard. You could hear chickens clucking and a cow moo every once in awhile. Old Alvin must a heard us coming, because he rushed out of the house carrying a shotgun.

"What're you doing here?" he shouted. "Go on, git off my land!"

"We've got a search warrant, Mr. Wilson," Jake called.

"I don't give a goddamn for your search warrant! Get outta here!" He fired the shotgun, which spooked the horses but did no damage as we were too far away. "There's your goddamned search warrant!" He broke the shotgun open and reloaded quickly.

"Don't make us shoot back, Mr. Wilson," Jake shouted. "We won't miss."

Wyatt slid his carbine out of his saddle holster, drew a bead, and cocked it. "I got him," he said.

"Don't shoot," I said. "I'll handle this."

"You'll what?" Jake exclaimed.

"I said I'll handle it!" I replied gruffly, the first time I ever took that tone with Jake. "I'll handle it," I said in a calmer voice. "He won't shoot me."

"The hell he won't," Jake said.

"The hell he will," I shot back. I jumped off my horse and called, "I'd like a word, Mr. Wilson."

Behind me, I heard Jake say to Wyatt, "He makes a move on Nate, put him down."

"He's all mine," Wyatt said.

"A word, Mr. Wilson," I said, walking toward him, "and nobody has to get hurt."

"Git outta here, and nobody will get hurt."

"Put down the shotgun, Mr. Wilson," I said, walking toward him. I should of been afraid out of my wits, walking toward an armed man like that, but I weren't. I just knew, don't ask how, that he wouldn't shoot me.

"I won't!" he said.

"You can't win, Mr. Wilson. That man with the Winchester aimed at your head back there? That's Wyatt Earp! Now, I'm wearin' a badge, he's wearin' a badge, and you got a gun on me. He could shoot you dead this very second, and the law would be on his side. Now, I don't want that, and you don't want that. So put down the gun."

He laid the shotgun across his shoulder. "You want to talk. So, talk."

"Where are your boys, Mr. Wilson?"

"They ain't here."

"Well, we know that. And I thought if they was smart they could be in Mexico by now, easy, and we'd just be wasting our time. The truth? That's what I thought until just now when you come out of the house with a shotgun. That changed my mind right quick. If they was in Mexico, you wouldn't be afraid for 'em. 'Stead a comin' out with a gun, you'd a had nothin' but your thumb on your nose, laughin' at us."

"Maybe I just don't like tinhorn lawmen on my land," he said.

"I'm really flattered you'd call *me* a lawman," I said. "I know how silly I must look, a fifteen-year-old kid wearin' a man's badge, carryin' a gun. But I can do a man's job. I've proved it. The trouble is, I ain't cut out to be a lawman. It ain't my style."

"Is that a fact? And why would I be interested, one way or t'other?"

"Because there's things a lawman has to do I don't like. I mean, besides killing. I've done that, too, thanks to you, and it don't sit well with me. Some fellers don't have no problem with it. I do. I don't like killin' nothin' if I can help it. Killed me a coral snake once. I was out near the mine—Ned Harper's mine. Oh, and did I ever tell you, I own a piece of it, too? Twenty-three percent."

"You what?" he hollered.

"Yeah, it's been great. I guess if it don't go bust, I'll be rich as you someday. Anyhow, I run into this coral snake, scared the bejesus outta me. I quick grabbed a stick and just beat the crap out of it till it was good and dead. Trouble was, I remembered too late—you know, the way you can tell if a coral snake is poisonous or not. You look at the stripes. 'Red touches yellow, you're a dead fellow; red touches black, you're all right, Jack.'

"Well, this poor snake had red touching black. And I killed it. Didn't mean me no harm, probably just as scared a me as I was of him. And I felt just awful about it—I mean, for days. So if I get all worked up over a snake, imagine how hard it is on me to kill a man.

"Well, I'm sorry, Mr. Wilson, I been runnin' off at the mouth again, prob'ly borin' you to death. But I spent fifteen years bein' told to shut up ever five seconds, and never talkin' much a'tall to begin with. I cleaned spittoons. Who'd a cared about anything I had to say? So I guess I'm makin' up for it now.

"What was I sayin'? Oh, yeah, about bein' a lawman. You know what else I don't like? Stickin' my nose in other people's business."

"That there's the first smart thing you've said," Wilson grumbled.

"I'm sure you're right. But what I was gettin' at was, I also don't like comin' onto other people's property without their welcome, even if I do have a warrant and the law says it's okay."

"Then what're you doin' here?"

"Well, this is a special case, Mr. Wilson. You want to know what makes it so special?"

"I'm breathless waitin'."

"You should be. Turns out, Mr. Wilson, that I can come on this land anytime I want. You wanna know why?"

"What the hell are you talkin' about?"

"Because this land ain't yours. IT'S *MINE,* you son of a bitch!" Before he could move, I jumped at him, ripped the shotgun from his hands, threw it away, and pushed him to the ground.

Jake, Wyatt, and Lida Mae leaped off their horses and run toward us.

"Nate! What's going on?" Jake asked.

I ignored him and drew two pieces of paper from my coat pocket. I backhanded the first one at Alvin; it fluttered to the ground next to him.

"You know what that is? It's my birth certificate. This should be a really big deal for me, and I can't understand it, but I don't care.

"*You* are my father, Mr. Wilson. But you knew that.

You always knew that, and it didn't mean nothin' to you. Well, you know what? I don't *want* you to be my father! I don't want to be anything like you. How good a father could you be, anyway? You raised five sons, and every one of them is a . . . worthless . . . *shithead!*" I looked around me, bewildered. "How did you do that? How did you manage to have five sons, and not a single decent thing about any one of them? You've got to work *hard* to pull that off."

Lida Mae came up behind me and put a gentle hand on my shoulder. "He had six sons, Nate," she said softly. "And everything that was good went into the last one."

I nodded my thanks to her. "So, Mr. Wilson . . . Alvin . . . *Daddy* . . . it turns out that I'm Nathaniel *Wilson.*" I shook my head quickly, like I'd just tasted something awful. "No. I don't like it. Nathaniel . . . Levy . . . I could stand that." I nudged Jake. "Nathaniel . . . Murchison . . . I like that, too. Even . . . Nathaniel . . . *Jenks* . . . is a step up. But I ain't now, and never was, Nathaniel Wilson."

Alvin got up slowly and brushed himself off. He looked at me with hate in his eyes. "That's right. You ain't a Wilson. You'll never be a Wilson."

"You low-down, scum-suckin' bastard," Wyatt growled at him. "Turn your back on your own kin! You oughta be horsewhipped. And I'd like to do it."

"He ain't no kin a mine," Alvin said. "I don't give a crap what that piece a paper says."

I laughed, but it wasn't the kind of laugh where something is funny. "I can't tell you how relieved I am to hear you say that," I said, "because it's gonna make what I got to say next that much easier." I held up the other piece of paper. "You wanna know what this is?"

"I don't give a rat's ass what it is," Alvin replied.

"Well, you're gonna. This here document, this one's even better than the last. This here's a gift from my mother. You know that mine that's made you so rich? Well, I didn't know this, I guess nobody did. My mother, Miss Flora Jenks, done lent you the money to buy into that mine."

"So what," Wilson said.

"So this. *You never paid it back.* And I'll bet you never gave her a nickel a the profits, either."

"Jesus!" Jake breathed.

"So what I got here is a note on your mine. A note that has long since been in foreclosure. And I'm calling it in . . . *now.*"

"That dirty whore!" Wilson shouted.

"Hey!" I shouted back. "Shut up! That 'dirty whore' loved you—don't ask me why. Why else would she forget the loan? Why else would she give herself to nobody but you all these years?" I thought for a minute and was hit hard with a realization. "And why else would she pretend I wasn't her son?" I calmed down. "You got rich off a whore, Alvin. What's that make you?"

"Well, I can pay that back now," Wilson said. "Hell, I damn near got that in my pocket!"

"It's too late," I said. "I got the right to foreclose. You got till tomorrow to get off this land. Right now, I'm going into your house—my house—and I'm seizing everything, all your ownership papers, all your stocks and bonds, and all your cash."

I started walking toward the house and stopped. "Oh. Jake, I'm sorry. I didn't mean to be rude. I know I shouldn't eavesdrop. But that time in your office, you gave Pappy here a—what was it? A restraining order. Can't you arrest him right now?"

"By God, he's right!" Jake said. "You are, perhaps indirectly, but nevertheless, partially responsible for the judge's murder. Marshal Earp, would you place Mr. Wilson in custody, please?"

"Be glad to," Wyatt said.

"You can't do this to me!"

"Then you tell us where your sons are!" I screamed into his face.

"They're at the mine!" he cried, crumpling. "They're hiding out at the mine!" He sat down and started to weep. "My boys! My house! My money!"

I knelt down on the ground next to him. "Alvin," I said softly. "Alvin. Listen to me. *Listen* to me. I'm *not* taking your house. I'm *not* taking your property. I don't want it. I never did."

"Piss on 'im," Wyatt said. "Take it. Take it all."

"You're not gonna?" Alvin said weakly. "You won't take my—"

"No. I don't want it," I said. "I don't want any part of you. You think I could live in that house? Keep it. And we're not going to arrest you. Even with the restraining order, I don't think you really wanted the judge killed. I'll bet you blew your stack when you found out about it."

"I-I d-did do that," he said.

"We don't really want Buck," I said. "Nor Virge, or even Bob. They're scared a Tad—hell, *I'm* scared a Tad—so they probably went along just 'cause he made them. So you won't lose them. Earl? Well, that was a pretty solid oak door. Earl's probably the only feller in the county strong enough to've kicked it in. But maybe he just figured Tad was goin' in to scare the judge, have a little fun makin' him squirm. Maybe when Tad's gun come out, he said, 'What the hell you doin'? I didn't come along for that!' So maybe he'll get off light. Wyatt? You know how it works better'n any a us. What do you think?"

"Christ, I'd hang the lot of 'em, it was up to me," he answered, "but figure the tub'll get five, maybe do a year, maybe the whole thing suspended, you pay off the right judge. Maybe the tub even tried to stop him, 'n maybe his brother drew on him and told him to shut up or he'd get some, 'n maybe the tub lit on outta there. All depends on what he says in court, 'n how greedy the judge is."

"What about my boy? What about Tad?" Wilson asked.

"Your favorite." I nodded.

"Tad goes down," Jake said quietly. "Assassinating—" He thought of the judge and gave a sad smile. "Assassinating a public official is a hanging offense. And this is two counts of murder. And it was premeditated; he went there with a gun. Maybe he didn't mean to use it—maybe he could try for manslaughter, he was drunk, he didn't know what he was doing, it's a tough call. But don't get your hopes up. He murdered a judge. What other judge will forgive that?"

"My boy!" Alvin cried. "Oh, my boy!"

"Alvin?" I said. "I'm sorry it worked out this way. But I've got one more thing to tell you. I told you I'm not taking this property. And I won't. But you're not keeping it all, neither. I know you'll be grievin' tomorrow, but you have no choice. Tomorrow, you'll go to the bank. Bring Mr. Stout the paper on everything you own and all of your cash. Then you're gonna sign one-half of it over to Flora Jenks."

"I . . . what?"

"She helped you . . . now you're going to help her. She gets half of everything, a new life out of the cathouse, and that's how you'll repay her. We'll tell Mr. Stout to expect you. And, Alvin, if you don't show up, we'll all come back and see to it that you do."

"I . . . have to do that?"

"Yes, you do," Jake said, putting an arm around me, "and you're getting off easy. For that you can thank the only thing in this world you can be proud of."

14

OUR RIDE TO the mine was far slower than the one out to the ranch had been. There was no hurry; the Wilson boys wasn't goin' nowhere. They could a been in Mexico hours before if they'd been smart, but they wasn't. They had noplace else to go.

The mine that I owned with Ned Harper was just that—a mine. A hole in a mountain and a little camping settlement for Emlyn and his boys.

Well, the Wilson mine was a lot more than that. It seemed to be a whole other town, maybe almost as big as Granger itself. He had hundreds of fellers working for him, living in these crumbly old shacks, a big smelting operation, and big tent set up where the boys et. And there wasn't just one mine. There was at least three that I could see, and they had little railroad cars set up on tracks that drove the ore right from the mountain into where it got smelted. But it was nighttime, and everything was still. I would a like to have seen this place during a workday—it must of been something to see.

"No wonder he's so damn rich," I said to Lida Mae as we rode in. "No tellin' what *we* could do with all this stuff."

"We'll get there, Nate," she said. "It'll just take us a little time."

"Say, where do you think you're goin'?" A voice called out.

"Who wants to know?" Wyatt replied.

A chubby old feller with a night watchman's hat and badge stepped out of the shadows. "I ain't supposed to let nobody in here," the night watchman said. "Orders from the boss."

"We've got a search warrant," Jake said.

"Give it here."

Jake took out the warrant and reached down, handing it to the watchman. The watchman took out a pair of spectacles and held it up to a nearby light.

"This here's jes' for Mr. Wilson's house," he said. "It don't say nothin' about searchin' no mine."

"It says 'property,'" Jake replied. "This is Wilson's property."

"Well, I would argue that," the watchman said.

"All right, you old coot," Wyatt said, "then try this. There's a murderer hiding out on this here property. We know it, and you know it. And if you try'n stop us, we'll run you in for aidin' and abettin' a lawbreaker. You wanna share a cell with 'im?"

The watchman looked at each of us for help, but there wasn't none coming.

"I know you're just trying to do your job, mister," Wyatt said in an easier tone. "But it ain't worth stickin' your neck out. So where are they?"

"Where's who?" the watchman asked, like he didn't know.

"You don't have to worry about your job," Jake said. "Mr. Wilson told us they'd be here. Now, what I suggest you do, sir, after you tell us exactly where to find them, you go into these shacks and tell the miners to stay inside where they'll be safe. Do that, and later we'll get together and cook up a story for Mr. Wilson that'll make you look like a hero."

"A hero?" the old feller perked up. "Like in the papers?"

"*Just* like the papers," Jake assured him. "Maybe we'll even get your name in."

"My name in the papers? Well, now, wouldn't that be a sight!"

"Where are they?" Jake asked again.

"They're in the number two mine, the one's been closed down for a bit."

"Closed down?" I asked. "What for?"

"Don't know much about it, young feller. Seems there's a sorta leak somewheres. Wouldn't do no shootin' in there, I was you. Place'd go off like a Roman candle on the Fourth a *Ju*-ly."

I tipped my hat. "Much obliged," I said.

"Name's Parsons," he called after us as we rode off, "Ewell Parsons! Make sure the papers git it right!"

We pulled up short of the entrance to the number two mine and dismounted. "Everybody wait here," Jake said. "I'm going in and check it out."

"I'll come with you, Jake," I said.

"So will I," Lida Mae said.

"I ain't twiddlin' my thumbs out here," Wyatt added.

"Wyatt," Jake said, "I need you out here in case they

get past me. Lida, you're not going in, and that's final."

She started to protest, but he cut her off. "Don't even bother, Lida. You're not going to win this one, so don't even try."

It surprised me, but she just nodded. She put her arms around him and kissed him. "Be careful," she said.

"Don't worry. Nate, I can't let you go in there, either."

"Well, I ain't lettin' you go in there alone."

"I can't shoot them, Nate," he said. "You heard what Parsons said."

"All the more reason why you need another hand," I said. "Jake, they're my *brothers.*"

"And what fine brothers they've been to you all these years."

"Jake, we're wastin' time. So unless you wanna flatten me right here and now, there's no other way to stop me."

"All right," Jake said. "What the hell. You wanted to be deputy, anyway."

"And he can talk a blue streak, just like you," Wyatt said. "So you might as well let him go along. When he was talkin' to old Wilson back there, I damn near surrendered to 'im myself."

"Let's go," Jake said.

We crept into the mine entrance, following the tracks. Our guns was drawn but not cocked 'cause we didn't want to take the chance of a accidental fire that could blow us all to kingdom come.

The mine entrance was held up with wood beams, and the path swooped up and down and this way and that. It was lit with these special kind a lanterns that wasn't supposed to expose the flame to the air, but they still made me nervous. I started sniffing, waiting to smell something that might be the leak.

"Jake," I whispered. "You hear somethin'?"

He didn't answer. "Jake?" I said again. "Jake?" But all I heard was a thump. Then I felt something slam me in the back of the neck, and that was the last thing I felt for what seemed like a long, long while.

When I come to, I found myself against a beam next to Jake. They'd taken our guns away, but they couldn't tie us up, not having any rope. All the Wilson brothers—*my* brothers—were huddled a bit away from us, probably figurin' on how to kill us. All except Earl. He was sitting on the ground by himself, not looking too much like his was a rosy world.

Jake didn't seem no worse for the wear except for some dry blood down the side of his face.

"You all right, Nate?"

"Been better," I said. My neck hurt like hell.

"Well, now, look who's awake," Bob said.

"You don't really resemble any of them, do you, Nate?" Jake asked me.

"Must be on account a my mother," I said.

"Whyn't you shut up," Bob said. "I still ain't forgotten about that time at Flora's. This oughta be fun."

"Come over here, Bob," Tad said. "Stop playing the fool."

"What do you boys have in mind?" Jake called over to them. "You know you're not getting out of here. Marshal Earp and another deputy have the entrance covered. And there's a posse on its way down from Granger."

"Shut up," Buck said.

"You were right, Nate," Jake said to me, as if no one else was listening. "They won't kill us. They can't. They need us to get out of here alive."

"The hell you say," Virge said.

"Well, you tell me, Virge. This is a mine—one way in, one way out. Wyatt Earp waiting for you right outside. What chance do you have without live hostages?"

"Maybe we only need one hostage," Buck said. "Who says it has to be you?"

"All right," Jake said agreeably, "let's say you have one hostage. You come out there, him in front, somebody muffs it, a shot goes off, the hostage gets killed. Now you have no hostages. How long you think you'll live after that?"

Nobody answered him. I sneaked a look over at Tad, the first time I'd seen him since the judge's murder. He didn't look good. His face was all pale and pasty, and his hands trembled. Once or twice, he made a face and put his fingers to his temples. That was how I knew that Tad was smack in the middle of a hangover could kill a horse. I knew about hangovers; I'd seen enough of 'em. I'd seen enough men wake up in jail, not a clue of what they'd done to get them in there in the first place.

"Say, Tad," I said. "You wanna feel better? Get a strong boy like Earl there to squeeze on your shoulders, make sure his thumbs gits the part between your shoulder blades. That helps a lot, I seen it myself."

If it'd been any other time, Tad mighta come over and kicked me in the head. Instead, he looked over at Earl and jerked his head.

But Earl wasn't goin' nowhere. "Do it yer own damn self," he said.

"I'll do it," Buck said. He got behind Tad and started kneading on his back. Tad made a pained face but then relaxed. "Ain't bad," he said.

"Might as well enjoy life while you can, Tad," Jake said.

"Oh? Why's that?"

"Oh, come on, Tad. Why'd you run away? Why are you hiding out in this hellhole?"

"I knew people'd blame me, that's why," he said. "That sumbitch Earp heard me tell the judge I'd get 'im. They knew I was mad 'cause I'd lost . . . the 'lection. Who else would they blame?"

"Who else is there, Tad? I mean, really, who else had a motive?"

"I didn't do it, and you couldn't prove it if I did." Buck's working on his shoulder was starting to help Tad feel better. "That's okay, Buck," he said. "Get me some water."

Buck nodded and reached for his canteen. Tad uncorked it, put it up to his mouth, and almost drained the whole thing.

"I think I can prove it, Tad. You're a fast gun, aren't you? First time I met you, you wanted to draw on me. I could tell from how scared everyone in the saloon was. Yeah, you must be a fast gun."

"So I'm a fast gun. So what?"

Jake stretched comfortably. "I don't know how much you really know about police work, Tad. I know you wanted to be marshal, but what do you really know about what it involves, besides ambling around town looking snotty? Well, it doesn't matter. What does matter is that I've been a policeman in a big city. Crime is different in the cities, Tad. I guess you've never lived in one. But it's different, all right. Not like here, where everyone knows everyone else and all their business. In the city, a cop on the beat can come across a dead body, and you have this small area, say, the size of Granger, but with thousands of people in it living right on top of each other. I don't think you'd like the city, Tad.

"Well, cities are getting bigger. And there's more and more crime. You find a dead man, it's not like here, where any one of a hundred people could say, 'Why, that's John Smith! He had a hell of a fight with Jim Jones last night, beat the crap out of him! I guess this is old Jim's way of paying him back.' And more often than not, they're right.

"No, Tad, it's not like that at all. You can search for days, sometimes weeks before you find one person who even knew the dead man. And only then can you start trying to figure out who killed him. You have to knock on doors. Talk to hundreds of people, find just one person who might've seen or even heard something. And then you have to hope that they remember it, that it even meant enough to them to recall it."

Jake stretched out again. "Damn! I wish I could smoke a cigar in here. Where was I? Oh, yes. Well, Tad, none of this works anymore. Well, why should it? The world's changing, growing up, progressing. How many trains were there in America fifty years ago? Was there such a thing as a telegraph? A six-gun? What I'm getting at is, police work has to catch up, too. That's why, in a lot of big cities, you don't have only regular policemen. There's a whole new aspect of police work, new types of police-men, and they're called detectives. Have you ever heard of them, Tad?"

"Whyn't you shut the hell up?" Bob sneered.

"Just passing the time," Jake said. "And I'm talking to Tad, here. He seems interested, aren't you, Tad?"

Tad didn't say anything, which Jake took for a yes. "So, Tad, we have detectives now. I ran a precinct, and I knew a few good ones. Most of them could size up a murder pretty well. Dead girl, very attractive, think jealous husband or sweetheart, and usually you were right. Dead rich guy, mean bastard, young wife, think wife and her lover. Again, you're usually right. Instinct helps a lot. So you bring a fellow in, and sooner or later, if you know which questions to ask—questions where you already *know* the answer—it's just a matter of time before your man confesses."

He pointed to Bob's canteen. "I don't suppose I could have some of that water, could I?" He shook his head to answer his own question. "No? Well, here in the West, Tad, maybe we don't need detectives just yet. The judges out here just aren't as demanding. Well, call me snooty, but they're not really judges, and they really don't have courts. What's the average courtroom out here? Somebody's general store or even a saloon. Not where I come from, Tad. The courthouses are like giant cathedrals! Kind of makes you respect the law more, because you take it a little more seriously. It's a much longer and involved process, Tad. And it's run by people who you don't know and don't know you. And when you bring in a man you think is guilty, well, you'd better present them with a case that's airtight, because they take the law seriously, too. If I arrest a man—even a man, who, like yourself, murders a judge—well, I'd better be able to prove he did it. Because if I didn't, I'd get taken apart on the stand and be made to look like the world's biggest imbecile.

"But New York isn't the Arizona Territory, Tad. I bring in a man for killing a judge, well, you don't have that complicated machinery of justice out here. You don't have those cathedral-type courthouse buildings and police forces with thousands of men. Out here, you've got maybe one judge for hundreds of square miles, and little towns with just one cop. If word gets out that somebody kills a judge, they can't take the chance that he's innocent. Which you're not. They can't take that chance at all. Because if you get away with it, then the next fellow will think he can get away with it, and before you know it, Arizona has no judges, no marshals, and no justice. Just a bunch of fast guns who shoot anybody who gets them mad and no one to rein them in."

"I toleja I didn't do it," Tad said.

"Of course you did, Tad. I know it, you know it, everybody here knows it, and by now, so does everyone in town."

"All right," Tad said. "Say I did do it—just *say* I did. Why are you telling me this? You're sayin' I'm gonna hang. Why the hell should I listen to you? What's in it for me?"

Jake shook his head, his famous head-clearing thing. "Oh, Tad, I'm sorry! Did you think I was telling you this to help *you?* I'd like to, but I'm not sure I can. No, I was concerned about your brothers."

"What the hell do you mean?" Buck demanded.

"Well, come on," Jake said, spreading his hands. "Remember, we've got a murdered judge . . . and let's not forget Irma. But, anyway, you've got a dead judge and five brothers who run away right after it happens. Why, you're all accomplices. I thought you knew that."

"I didn't do nothin'!" Virge shouted. "I wasn't even there!"

"Shut up, Virge," Bob said, smacking him on the side of the head.

"None of that matters, Virge. You're here, aren't you? What's a real judge going to think?"

"Tad's in trouble, is all," Buck said. "We didn't say he did it. We're just standin' by him 'cause he's our brother. We Wilsons stick together!"

"Really," Jake said. "That's funny, because I also know that isn't true."

"What you mean, it isn't true?"

"Because you've got another brother, and you've always treated him like a dog."

"What're you talkin' about?"

"Nate. Nate here's your brother."

"The hell you say! That little—"

"He's your brother; watch what you say."

"Nate's our brother?" Virge squeaked.

"Bull," said Bob. "Who's his mother? Not ours!"

"No, it's Miss Flora. I assure you, it's true. Nate's birth certificate is in his saddlebag."

"So his mother's a whore! I figgered as much!" Buck said.

"And his father is your father," Jake said.

"You're my brother?" Virge said to me.

"Yeah," I said, "but it don't make me want to get up and dance."

"Get back over here, Virge!" Bob shouted.

"No, wait," Virge said. "You're my kid brother?"

"Yeah," I said.

"Well, I'll be go to hell! I ain't the goddamn runt a the litter no more!" He punched me in the shoulder.

"He ain't no brother of ours," Bob spat.

"He's got a birth certificate," Virge said.

"Don't matter! He ain't our brother!"

"But he is! What the hell's the matter with you?"

Bob ran over and smacked Virge again, really hard this time. "Look here, stupid! Our daddy done screwed a whore! She had a kid, 'n that's him! That *don't* make him our brother!"

"Then why do I feel bad?" Virge shouted back.

Bob grabbed Virge by his collar. "You with us? Or you with him? Now git the hell back!" He threw Virge across the room. Virge landed hard, the wind knocked out of him.

"Nice family you've got there," Jake said to me out of the side of his mouth.

"I always thought so," I whispered back.

"Well, now, boys," Jake said, "it warms my heart to see a close family together. So I take it you're all ready to hang."

"We ain't gonna hang," Buck said.

"Yes, you are, and I'll tell you why. You all rode over to the judge's house together. Even though the three of you, Buck, Bob, and Virge, all stayed outside, you're still part of what is called a conspiracy. You all knew Tad's intent, and still you went with him. Maybe in New York you'd get off with a prison sentence, but here in Arizona? Examples must be made. Earl? You've been pretty quiet. I guess you know you're finished, too. You used that great strength of yours and booted that door right open. The jamb was a mess, Earl. No one but you could have done that. Tad? I doubt you really would have killed him if you weren't so drunk and so mad. But you're a hell of a shot, drunk or sober. It was the nick in Irma's shoulder that proved it to me. Think about it: Boom, the first shot to the judge's chest, Irma tries to take it herself, and you get that next shot off so fast you almost get the judge again in the same spot. Irma can't even throw herself across him fast enough to take it full in the back like the other two.

"Then, with the job done, and your brothers terrified—they probably said, 'You did what?'—you probably went home and told your father what you did. I'll bet he smacked every one of you, and shouted and cursed and called you idiots, but then his fatherly love took over. 'Go to the mine,' he said. 'Hide out there until I can clear this up.' I guess he figured Mexico was too dangerous, too many bounty hunters. The five of you together would have been easy to spot.

"Well, boys, that's what'll be in my report. It's too bad, but the four of you really didn't have to hang along with Tad. The three of you who weren't inside? You really didn't know what was going to happen. Just tell the judge you can't believe he did something like that. You thought he was just going there to talk. Why, you might not have even been charged.

"Earl? It's true you forced the door, but so what? Breaking and entering? Nothing. A suspended sentence. Maybe six months in the territorial prison if a judge is having a bad day. But if you show that you tried to stop Tad and were placed in fear for your life, even the toughest, meanest judge couldn't do much to you."

Earl had been sitting on the floor with his head in his hands. "It weren't right," he said.

"No, Earl, it wasn't."

"I never should a done that," Earl said. "I didn't think Tad would shoot him."

"One question, Earl," Jake said, "and you might as well answer it, because they'll ask you in court. You're twice as big as Tad. You're the strongest man in town. Tad was drunk. Why didn't you just coldcock him, throw him over your shoulder, and carry him out of there?"

Earl shook his head. "I don't know. I never done hit Tad afore. Never woulda thought of it."

"Marshal?" It was Tad. "Marshal, lemme ask you somethin'."

"Sure, Tad."

"If I say I done it . . . and my brothers had nothin' to do with it . . . and then I ran away and they follered me here and was all tryin' to convince me to turn myself in . . . would you let 'em go?"

"No, Tad!" Buck shouted.

"Shut up, Buck. Would you do it, Marshal?"

"What about the door, Tad?"

"Say I shot it open."

"There're no bullets in or near the door."

"Well, then I was drunk. I kicked it myself. You seen men do things drunk they can't do when they's sober."

"Jake?" I said. "What do you think?"

Jake thought for a moment. "All right, Tad."

"Don't do it, Tad!" Bob cried.

"Gotta do it, Bob. Ain't no choice. I ain't lettin' my brothers hang for me. Okay, Marshal? We got a deal?"

"We've got a deal." Jake stood up, walked over to Tad and held his hand out. Tad took his gun out of its holster and handed it over.

"You boys all give Nate and me your gun belts."

There was some protest from Bob and Buck, but Earl shut them up. "Take off them damn gun belts," Earl growled, and they did. Virge didn't argue at all.

"All right," Jake said. "I want you boys to walk slowly outside. Put your hands up high. Marshal Earp will be out there, along with Deputy Harper, and you want to be sure they don't start shooting. They're both crack shots."

Virge went out first. After a bit, Earl shoved Bob hard,

and Buck even harder. Then he raised his hands and began to follow them out.

"All right, Tad, let's go," Jake said.

"Uh, Marshal?" Tad said. "Can I talk with Nate for a minute?"

"Outside," he said.

"It's private," Tad insisted.

"What for?"

"It's private. Might be my only chance ever to talk with my brother."

"It's okay, Jake," I said. "He won't do nothin'. Please."

"I guess you know what you're doing." Jake sighed. "All right, a minute. Then I come back in and drag you both out. And remember our deal, Tad. Anything happens to Nate, it's off. Keep that in mind."

"Nothin'll happen to Nate."

Tad and I just looked at each other while Jake turned and walked out. Then Tad reached in his pocket and took out a flask.

"Drink with me, little brother."

"Sounds funny, comin' from you." I took the flask and was about to sip from it when something struck me. "You *knew*," I said. "You *always* knew."

"Wish my other brothers was smart as you," Tad said. "Wouldn't a winded up like this."

"How did you know? I know your father thought you were the only worthwhile one in the bunch, but still, he'd never a told you *that*."

Tad took the flask from me, took a slug, and handed it back. "He never done told me. He don't know I know."

"How'd you find out?"

"You wasn't the only smart Wilson, Nate," he said. "Daddy was bughouse over Flora. Or, no offense, maybe bughouse over the way she screwed. I was a kid, what six, seven years old. Never could sleep. Hated the dark. Usedta git up 'n sneak around. Daddy usedta wait till my ma fell asleep. Real late, like after midnight, he'd git up, go out to the barn. Never knew why. But it happened a lot. Two, three times a week. Ain't you gonna drink with me, brother?"

I took a sip, my first ever. And one of my last. I handed him back the flask.

"Always wondered," Tad said, "what was in that damn barn needed his attention that late at night. So, one night, I get up the guts, sneak on out, and peek between a couple loose boards. Want to know what I saw?"

"I think I got a pretty good idea."

"Yeah, my daddy 'n your mama, humpin' to beat the band. I guess that's where you was made . . . in our barn."

"Figures I was made in a barn," I said. "Figures that's why I was right at home livin' in one all those years."

"You know what got me? You know what I think Daddy really liked about your ma? I done watched 'em plenty a times after that, and they done everything, but one thing stays in my head most. When they'd be doin' it normal, Flora'd be kissin' Daddy the whole time. Like she'd never take her mouth from his for two seconds if she could help it."

I nodded. "Yeah. She loved him, all right. Enough to do whatever he asked. Damned if I know why."

"Yeah. He's a ugly old bastard, ain't he?" Tad said and started to laugh. I joined in, and soon our laughter was ringing through the mine. I wondered what they was thinking outside.

"Anyhow, once I heard 'em a-fightin'. Not yellin' or nothing. But Daddy talking real low, real mad, 'n Flora cryin'. Then Flora didn't never come after that."

"That's where I come in, I guess."

"Sorry I been a shit to you, Nate," he said. "Sorry, but I don't know, if I had it to do over, I'd probably do the same. Don't know why."

"Forget it," I said. "It's done."

"Yeah," he said. "And so am I." He reached behind him into his belt and took out something black. "Yeah," he said. "So am I. I never meant to kill nobody, Nate."

"Don't much matter now, Tad."

"No. I suppose it don't."

I wasn't surprised to see that the black thing was Jake's gun, the second gun he had always carried. Tad must have taken it off of him when they conked us. Jake had been wearing it so long he probably didn't notice it one way or t'other.

I wasn't afraid. I knew the gun wasn't for me.

Tad held up the flask in his other hand. "Have another slug," he said. "Then say good-bye to your big brother."

"Okay." I held up the flask, like to say cheers, and took a long draught. "There's still some left," I said.

"Give it here."

"I guess this is it," I said.

"Guess you're right. You'll tell Jake, go easy on my brothers—our brothers—won't you? Hangin' just ain't my style."

"Sure, Tad. Well, I'd shake hands or somethin', but . . . I've hated your guts all these years." I couldn't help chuckling when I said that.

"Never hated you, Nate," he said. "Never hated nobody. Just never cared one way or the other."

"I figured as much."

"Well, good-bye, Nate. You'd best go on."

"So long, Tad."

He was draining the flask as I turned and walked away. Only when I was out of his sight did I start to run.

I heard the shot when I reached the mine entrance. And then there was a second of nothing, then a loud rumble, and then a terrific, invisible, giant fountain of air shot me out of the mountain like a ball from a cannon.

15

I SHOULD A been dead, of course, but I weren't, as you can see. I didn't feel awful good for the next few weeks. I stayed in bed, with Becky and her ma nursing me back to health and Jake never far away. He felt pretty bad about me almost getting blowed sky high, but I told him forget it. Wyatt Earp had stayed awhile, too, but was soon off on other business, as the shootings of the men who killed his brother Morgan would later tell us.

I didn't break no bones or nothin' when I come down, but I never did hear much outta my left ear, ever again. Doc Hayes was worried about somethin' called internal bleedin', which is where you bleed from the outside in instead of the inside out, and he kept saying there was no logical reason for me not to be deader'n Abe Lincoln. (Told you it was a Southern town.) But in spite a all he said, I got better anyhow.

The Wilson brothers was never charged with nothing. Everyone figured that since Tad blowed himself up along with the number two mine, everything was squared all around. The Wilson brothers never bothered nobody again; it was as if without Tad, they was a snake without no head, flopping around harmless-like, all the poison cut out of them.

Alvin Wilson paid Mr. Stout's bank a visit just like we told him to. It had been a rough time for him; the loss of his favorite son, one of his mines, and half his worldly goods. He signed Flora over her share, went on home, got into bed, and never stood, walked, nor said a word ever again. Doc Hayes called it a massive stroke. His four surviving sons was at sixes and sevens, nothing to do and no way of knowing how to do it. Their brother was gone, and now their daddy was almost gone, just a vacant pair a eyes, couldn't say nothing or move nothing.

Finally, of all people, Miss Flora took charge. She just moved herself into the house, hired on full-time nurses, and kept up the household. She spent much of the time reading to old Alvin and just keeping him company. I once asked her, didn't she feel odd about movin' into that house, and she said she should of, but it somehow felt natural as pie, like she belonged there. Even the boys didn't say nothin' about it; I guess they was glad to have someone to tell 'em when dinner was ready. Anyhow, Flora owned half of it, so she might as well of lived there.

The silver run out five years later. First Wilson's mine dried up, then Ned's. Didn't matter much to me by then, because I'd had most of my money invested in other things.

Didn't bother Ned much at all, neither. I don't think, as rich as Ned ever got, he ever felt like he really belonged in a frock coat with a silk cravat and a diamond stickpin. For Ned, the real fun was in the search, the digging, and the discovery. Him, Fred, Whitetail, and Emlyn

Jones and some a his best Welshmen all became a sort of gang. Once they showed up anywhere, there was suddenly silver or gold to be found. They kept moving, place to place, finding the treasure, getting it started, and moving on to a newer place, descending like a whirlwind, only kicking up gold and silver dust instead of dirt. They made all of us rich, and themselves even richer, though for those fellers, money was always the least of it.

Their headquarters was Tucson, where Jake and Lida Mae had a fine house. Jake stayed in Granger for another few years after he married Lida Mae. The legend of Gentleman Jake Murchison only grew up later on, when he was elected sheriff of Pima County, a job he held more than twenty years. During that time, he became famous for introducing modern police methods, including the first criminal fingerprint file in the territory.

Once the silver dried up, the town fizzled along with it. I went with the Levys to check on opportunities in San Francisco, a beautiful place, to be sure. But we had lived in Arizona too long, and the desert had thinned our blood. None of us could stand the cold, damp climate, so we wound up coming back in a hurry.

Me and Becky was able to stand it only another year and a half before we up and got married. We was still too young, but we was healthy and loved each other, and before long, we knew we'd better get married while we still wanted to, or soon we'd wind up getting married 'cause we *had* to. So at seventeen, we tied the knot and never looked back since. True to her word, Becky indulged me in my game of catch-up with my lost childhood, without one word of complaint, even when I became the first man in the state of Arizona to own his own automobile, his own motorcycle, his own JN2 Jenny aeroplane, and his own locomotive, all at the same time.

I still had one more big laugh coming before I settled down for good. Miss Flora died just before the silver run out—not a month after old Alvin breathed his last—and damned if she didn't up and leave everything she owned to me.

All of which meant that I owned the Wilsons' mine, half their house, and half their ranch. And what else I didn't know was that Flora had a bigger piece of the saloon and casino than Tom Tryer himself—so I owned that, too.

Well, a last laugh is a laugh, and you can bet I enjoyed it, but when I was done, I sold off everything. I didn't want no part of running it. When Becky and I got married, we moved to Tucson, right near Jake and Lida Mae, and that was where we stayed and raised our kids. The town where we had growed up just became another one of dozens of ghost towns that you might find anywhere in Arizona—towns that sprung up from nowhere, had a brief, rich life, and then just as quickly vanished back into nowhere. Vanished so completely that no matter how hard you strain your ears, you don't hear nothin' but the wind passing through. Even the ghosts have moved on.

Arizona became a state in 1912, and I served a couple terms in the state senate, along with, of all people, Virge Wilson, the only one of the remaining brothers who stayed in Arizona. The other three just took their money and scattered, but Virge married a nice girl, settled in Benson, and found out that with a good wife and a couple kids to love him, he was a pretty decent feller at the bottom. We never became close, but we did become friends, and Virge always said he was glad he had some family left in Arizona.

I guess the only other thing left for me to clear up happened just before Becky and I got married. In all the hubbub you always get before a wedding, we almost forgot about it and was damn near marching to the altar when it hit us both.

What was my name?

Well, it couldn't be Wilson, and Rebecca begged my pardon but said she wouldn't take it if it was. It also couldn't be Jenks. Flora had been nice enough to me before she died, but there was still a matter of fifteen years that wasn't about to go away.

I asked Jake what he thought, and then I asked Aaron what he thought, and they both told me pretty much the same thing. Take the name that fits around you like a warm blanket on a cold night; a name that says who you are and what you come from. And that was when I knew; there was only one name for me, and it had been there all along. It told the world exactly who I was and what I came from. I've worn it proudly ever since, and so has Rebecca and all our kids.

The Granger family.

PETER
BRANDVOLD

GENE SHELTON

"Shelton skillfully blends historical figures and actual events with made-up characters and imaginary situations."—*The Dallas Morning News*

__TASCOSA GUN

0-425-17257-0/$5.99

__MANHUNTER:

THE LIFE AND TIMES OF FRANK HAMER

0-425-15973-6/$5.99

No one knows the American West better.

JACK BALLAS

☐ *THE HARD LAND*

0-425-15519-6/$5.99

☐ *BANDIDO CABALLERO*

0-425-15956-6/$5.99

☐ *GRANGER'S CLAIM*

0-425-16453-5/$5.99

The Old West in all its raw glory.